ENDGAME

A DARK MAFIA ROMANCE - (NEVER BEEN CAUGHT 5)

IVY WONDER

CONTENTS

PROLOGUE

Derek

*D*ate: March 14, 2019

Location: Baltimore, Maryland

Subject: Adrian DuBois

Criminal Record: [Classified. D.D.: Please fill in any pertinent details using assistant director-level access as mine is insufficient].

Adrian Michel DuBois's actual background is unknown. Of the narratives about him that we were able to gather, three stand out as most likely.

One: He is of French-Canadian origin, is linked with the Sixth Family, and has built his fortune and influence through mob connections.

Two: He is the unacknowledged son of a French billionaire and has blackmailed this man into providing seed money for his ventures.

Three: He is a completely self-made man of Cajun descent who had executed several hacks against financial institutions to gain his seed money.

Whatever the case, our concrete knowledge of this subject is limited to a few photographs, his name, and a handful of facts.

One: He lives in the Baltimore area and may have family there.

Two: He is independently wealthy, has beyond genius-level intelligence, and has extensive underworld connections worldwide. This makes him a valuable potential asset, but also highly dangerous.

Three: Although he has been implicated in everything from racketeering to high-level computer crimes, there has never been sufficient evidence or any witnesses to convict him for a single charge.

"Yeah, honey, and you're not gonna be the one to change that." I chuckle, paging back through the thin notes and handful of photographs that are all my annoying bitch of an investigator got for me on DuBois. The classified stuff that she doesn't have access to—but I do—isn't much. Just some key details that I'm mostly planning to leave out, so she won't be forewarned.

Details like: DuBois is suspected to be behind the assassination of multiple high-ranking politicians and captains of industry. He's got whole crime families in his pocket. Politicians. Police departments.

In the FBI, ignorance of just how bad the bad guys are can be deadly. I'm going to make sure that she'll not only fail the investigation but endanger herself in the process. If I'm lucky, DuBois will straight up take out the trash for me.

Carolyn Moss. All pride, no practical ambition, no willingness to play the game she needs to play to keep my interest.

And keeping my interest was her one shot at getting anywhere under my management. But she couldn't even do that. And now someone in this office has told on me to both my superiors and my soon-to-be ex-wife ... and it was probably Carolyn.

And I'm going to use DuBois to make her pay for it.

DuBois is a genuine epic-level international crime lord with neither a criminal record nor anything else to hinder his constantly expanding power. He's surrounded by rumors, as Moss has learned, and he's both richer and more powerful than most legit billionaires in the States.

There is absolutely no fucking way she can catch DuBois, let alone bring him to trial. She's already failed to catch the other four; she's just been incredibly lucky, having managed to catch just enough criminals peripheral to those cases to keep me from writing her up. But now, her luck is bound to run out.

The plan's simple. Send her up there with little clue, no backup (as usual), and little support or intelligence. Have her annoy DuBois by sticking her nose into his business, and then have her either get terrorized enough to quit the Bureau or conveniently die.

Either way, she'll disappear out of my life forever. Probably after suffering horribly for a few days. And rumors have a certain way of scaring people into refusing to testify.

Once their ringleader is gone, those other bitches in the office will drop their beefs against me. They'll refuse to cooperate with the investigation, and I'm sure it will go away then.

Hard to understand why one of the other guys hasn't already murdered Moss yet. I handpicked them from the FBI's database of the most-deadly suspected cop killers in the United States. Not that I told her that.

When I ordered my computer guy to run a search for the worst of the worst, I also told him to rewrite some of their histories to make them look more harmless. He also gave me the copies of the original files in order to give me a look at what I was sending her against. These guys are monsters.

I gave her some line about how they were simply unusually hard to catch, so her pride and her desire to make her mark at the Bureau would needle her into stepping into their gunsights. Then I sent her out and waited for her to fail or die.

And yet every single goddamn time, she's come back almost completely unharmed. The worst thing that's happened to her has been jetlag and being snowed in once. I don't know how she constantly manages to avoid getting killed. It's like she has a guardian angel.

Meanwhile, she's made all kinds of trouble for me while I've been waiting for her to get killed like the reckless, untalented rookie girl she is. But her ability to cause more problems for me is about to come to an abrupt end.

I go back over what she's written and the section she's left blank for me. I consider typing in something misleading that fits with the rest it.

Something that makes it look like she made a mistake. Looked in the wrong file. Even made something up. Anything to make it look like what I want: that she's died from her own incompetence. After all, nobody needs to know that she asked me to write some of this.

It's not enough to get her out of my hair and out of the FBI. She also needs to pay, in pain and humiliation, for refusing to put out.

But to do that, I have to figure out how to fill this form's section, and my mind's a complete blank.

I sit back in my chair, rolling my eyes. How the hell does that woman even compile all this crap into a short narrative? Maybe I should keep her around after all—as my secretary.

But only if she finally decides to be full service like a good girl.

My guffaw fills my cramped office, and the custodian cleaning the other side of the outer office looks up briefly. He's some anonymous-looking guy in a uniform, like the five or six others I've seen. He's in nights, ironically always at around the same time that I stay late every night to get my revenge where no one can see.

I'd be more worried about that, but the guy's a fucking janitor. Even if he took a look at my office files or got into my computer, what are the chances that he would even know what he was looking at?

I know that the section director would come down on me like a mountain of bricks if he realized what I was doing with company resources on company time. But that bastard's wife is young and hot. He has no business judging men who don't have his luck.

If he wasn't getting laid, he would understand what a man feels driven to when he can't even get pussy from his fucking subordinates.

But now Carolyn Moss went and ratted me out for "sexual harassment." So now, it's not enough for her to get hurt, fail, and look like an idiot. She needs to die.

DuBois is going to be my red right hand this month, clearing the world of a pesky little bitch. And she has no idea what's coming.

CHAPTER 1

Carolyn

*T*here's a thunderstorm hanging low over Baltimore when I finally cart my suitcase and carry-on into my hotel room. The flash from a lightning bolt startles me as I push the door closed with my elbow. I jump slightly, then sigh and drop my bags, leaning against the door.

That wasn't even that long of a flight, but I'm beat. There was a three-hour delay because of the storm; we ended up landing in DC and riding over on a shuttle. Now, watching hail smack the big plate-glass window against the backdrop of a deep gray sky, I'm just glad it's not snow.

It's been a hell of a winter. I've been snowed in in Massachusetts, gone way outside my jurisdiction into Canada and Mexico, seen what happens when mobsters get into a chase with a crack driver on an icy road, and driven across a border with an assassin turned duct-tape mummy in my trunk. And four damn times, I've watched bad guys turn into heroes on me, confusing the hell out of me in the process.

It's not good to have a lot of internal debate about law and morality when you're a special agent of the FBI. Especially when you're new and have a million other problems to deal with, including a boss who seems to be out to get you. But the more I've been out here investigating these cases on my own, the more I've seen all the nuances that they don't teach you at Quantico.

My job is to take criminals in and clear cases. But I keep being thrust into situations where doing things the way my immediate boss expects will either get me killed or send a better person to jail while a worse person walks away. It's messing with my head.

Prometheus only adds to my confusion. He's my hacker contact whose intel and warnings have helped me stay alive and employed—but God only knows how many federal and local laws he's broken while doing that for me. People in law enforcement often look the other way about minor crimes in exchange for information ... but I don't think Prometheus's crimes are minor.

Still, between him and my boss, I know which one acts like he cares about me and which seems to be, not only out to get me, but irrational and corrupt. I just hope Derek Daniels goes down for his sexual harassment issues soon. I'm tired of him.

Instead of first checking in with him, I send a text to Prometheus via our secure line.

Made it in. Thank you for upgrading my hotel room.

The deluxe suite is way above grade compared to what Daniels often sticks me with. I'm warm enough for the first time since Mexico, the window doesn't rattle in its frame when the wind hits it, and the bed is large enough. My hair's already drying—well, except for the braid, which will be damp for hours.

I got the message about the upgrade barely half an hour ago, while I was still waiting to pick up my rental car. It came in suddenly and unexpectedly. Maybe it was just Prometheus letting me know that he knew I was in town. Or maybe he had a less show-offish motive for having me change rooms.

Any particular reason for the unexpected gift?

Still no answer. I order up a room-service chicken piccata and set up my remote office on the room's properly large desk. I have my laptop powering up and coffee perking when my phone rings.

I pick it up without looking at the number. "Hey, I didn't expect a phone call."

"Why wouldn't you?" Daniels grumps, startling me. "You haven't checked into your hotel room yet and it's nearly three in the afternoon."

I freeze for a moment, then draw a steadying breath and respond evenly. "I just barely walked in ten minutes ago."

"Hardly an excuse. Are you set up in 401 yet?"

I pause, finding it odd that he named my old room number. Normally he doesn't seem to pay any attention to small details like that. "They had a ceiling leak from the bathroom upstairs and are shuffling me into another room."

I hear a muffled curse.

"Sir?" I venture.

"Fine. Give me your new room number." He goes quiet, clicking away at his keyboard, and suddenly my stomach flutters with apprehension.

I give the number of one of the other suites the receptionist told me was vacant. I don't know why I don't give him the real number, but when I consider it, all my words stick in my throat. Has he shattered our trust that deeply? "407."

Maybe I should put in for a transfer once this is over.

"Fine. I sent you the updated profile on DuBois. Have a look at it and get started as soon as you can." He hangs up, leaving me listening to an empty line with my heart pounding.

What's he up to now? What's so special about 401? Maybe I should check it, if they haven't rented it out already.

I have no idea what I would find if I searched the place—or what I should even be looking for. But my training is telling me that something's wrong.

Then again, when it comes to Daniels, little is right. So, I might be paranoid about him to begin with ... but that doesn't mean I shouldn't check the room.

I leave a call at the front desk asking someone to let me into 401, claiming I accidentally had my luggage sent up to it. While I'm waiting for them or for Prometheus to contact me, I boot up my laptop and check out what Daniels has sent me.

I frown as I stare at the document. He has always instructed me to come to him if I can't retrieve the information I need from Bureau files. The details on DuBois's criminal history and international crimes were passworded; when I tried to access them, I got a notice telling me that the information was available to assistant directors and above only. So, I filled in as much as I could and then sent him a request for the additional information.

Now, after leaving me waiting for two days, all he has for me is a pair of thin paragraphs. Fuck you, Daniels. Are you holding out on me, or are you just lazy?

Little is known about Adrian DuBois's crimes due to a great deal of missing or expunged data on both American and international law enforcement sites. It is suspected that bribery or blackmail of inside sources was involved.

DuBois is not known to be involved in any violent crimes and is largely implicated in theft of property and information.

"That's nowhere near good enough," I grumble, but know it's all I have to work with. I have a handful of businesses to visit which are supposedly owned by DuBois under assumed names, and I have whatever Prometheus can get me, and that's it. And Prometheus has been quiet online since I got on the plane in Detroit.

It's strange. In a couple of months, I've started to feel closer to a man I've never met than I have to any man ever. Of course, with my background, that's no surprise. In my law enforcement and military family, Dad wanted nothing but sons.

He got six daughters in six tries and hates all of us.

Having a dad who won't even look at you, five sisters who take their self-loathing out on you and each other, and a mother who gave up and left after twenty years of trying, all take their toll. I have avoided any intimacy with men my whole life—partly to avoid more pain and partly because I have no idea how to deal with the whole complex social game of dating.

I can track fugitives with minimal clues, psychologically profile someone and often predict their next moves without ever meeting them and outsmart a boss who seems determined to get me fired. But figuring out how to find a good man may be beyond me.

I suppose that's how I ended up developing a tremendous crush on a man whose voice I have now heard, but whom I have never seen. Not because of lack of trying, however; I spent an extra month in Detroit looking for Prometheus after learning he was working with a local underground boxing ring's owner.

He refused to meet with me, even insisting once that it was for my own safety. Now, I'm up against a criminal mastermind so mysterious that even my boss knows precious little more than the rumors and anecdotes I'm working from.

I switch to the file attachments and open them, bracing myself. I've been avoiding looking at this set of file attachments in my assigned

11

series of five criminals ever since I first opened it—and it's because of his photographs.

All the men I've been chasing have been sexy as hell, along with being somehow both criminals and good men. I doubt the second trait will be true with DuBois, but as for the first ... he's the crown jewel of them all.

DuBois looks aristocratic—that's the right word. Tall, lean, polished, poised, his keen dark gray eyes are slightly crinkled at the corners and narrow with thoughtfulness. He has aquiline features, coal-black hair swept back from a high forehead, and in two of the photos, a little crystal cordial glass in his long-fingered hand.

He's the kind of man who can wear a signet ring and make it look not only good, but fitting. I stare at him and my face gets hot; I can't even make eye contact with a photo of him.

How in the world am I going to deal with the real thing?

There's only one possible way, since I'm without backup. Get close to him, meet other people close to him, and gather as much information as I can. Infiltrating his organization could take me months, but I don't care. I'm not giving up—and with the sexual harassment hearing against Daniels going on in the meantime, I'll be better off well away from New York City.

There are two ways to get close to him: seduction, which is risky and not my bag, or playing the desperate, corrupt FBI agent trying to get on his payroll. Feign some helplessness and shattered innocence for him to exploit, come in dragging a broken wing from, say, being betrayed and harassed by my sexist boss.

That makes me smirk. That works. I won't even have to make anything up. Except, of course, my motives.

I took an oath to uphold the law. But the more I go on, the more I see the difference between a clunky, antiquated system of laws that badly needs modernization and actual justice. I want to uphold what is right

—not just what the bureau, the government, and the courts have decided is most expedient.

Then I have a boss who likes to throw any sense of right and wrong out the window, and it's made the schism even more obvious. I still have to perform to the best of my ability in spite of Daniels, or I'll end up washing out of the job altogether. I'm under scrutiny thanks to him, and it's pushed me to do some pretty crazy things just trying to keep myself in the bureau's good books as an agent who clears cases and brings in perps.

I don't know how much more of this I can take if he doesn't leave the bureau soon. I just hope that his replacement is a better person to work with.

But meanwhile, I have to just keep struggling.

My phone buzzes at me. A text. It's Prometheus.

No real time to talk right now. I am in transit. I'm sending a courier with a piece of equipment for you that will answer your question about the sudden change of venue. Though I do prefer you to be comfortable, I also prefer that your private time in your hotel room be genuinely private. Expect the courier in twenty minutes.

I frown, text him a thank you, and start going through my notes on DuBois again. I guess asking Prometheus about the man of the hour will have to wait until he gets where he's going.

But I wonder what the hell is so urgent that he's sending a courier. What is he sending me and why?

CHAPTER 2

Adrian

"*H*ow was New York?" Marissa brings me my sweet tea as my private plane levels off over JFK. She's small and delicate-featured, with brown eyes and a severe black bob. The hairstyle and her trim black suit make her look closer to thirty, but she's twenty-three and has spent almost ten years trying to impress me when she's not teasing me.

When I found out that my father had impregnated one of our maids after Mother's death, I went looking for my discarded half-sister. I found her in a dingy foster home, took her in, and paid for her education. She's tremendously loyal and just as clever as me.

I pluck the lemon slice off the rim of the glass and squeeze it into my drink. "Dreary, dear sister, and boring. But our sources have now completed their task." I drop the twist of lemon rind into the drink and take a swallow, feeling the inside of my lips prickle a bit. Perfect.

"Including the janitor?" She flashes an impish grin as she settles onto the couch across from me, cradling her own glass.

"Yes. He now has copies of every one of Daniels's files, and has also copied his hard drive contents, which I will be looking at as soon as we arrive." My lips twitch with amusement. "I just sent him a nice bonus to cover the extra risk."

"Putting his kids through college?"

"Paid off his mortgage. He's single." I take another slow sip. My sweet tooth is my great weakness—aside from sentiment, of course.

"Probably worth it, if we can take this creep down. Even looking at his photo makes me want to punch him in the teeth. Ugh." She sets aside her drink and props her chin on her hands. "So …"

She grins slowly and I brace myself, knowing that I have some teasing coming. She's the only person in the world who gets away with it—and unfortunately, she loves to exploit that privilege.

"Go on, then."

"Are you going to go see this federal agent woman face to face or just keep moping over her?" Her nose wrinkles with mischief as I turn an annoyed look on her.

"I do not mope," I say a bit stiffly. Brood, consider, occasionally lie awake at night thinking—even with another woman sleeping beside me. But my interest in the lady in question must remain purely professional.

I don't ever allow myself to commit to long-term relationships with women due to the security concerns involved. Having a long-term lover or wife around is a point of vulnerability in both my security and my life, and I allow as few of those as possible. If I'm caught, it will interfere with my life's work, and that can't happen.

My standards for a long-term, committed partner are so high that I never even expected anyone to meet them. Then I learned of Special

15

Agent Carolyn Moss ... and found myself starting to reconsider, especially after we made contact.

I have grown closer to her, despite myself. I've even allowed her to hear my voice more than once.

That is all dangerous, and I've preoccupied myself with sorting out how to fix it without abandoning her or allowing her to come to harm. Both of those outcomes are unacceptable to me.

There is the possibility of adding her to my network, and thus my payroll ... but that depends entirely on her.

My original goal in reaching out to her was to prevent a terrible injustice instigated by her scheming superior who was literally attempting to lead her into either a humiliating failure at her job—or death. He's still doing it, and I'm still working to stop him. But somewhere along the way, things started getting personal.

I'm only human. But I have to be better than that.

"You're doing it again," Marissa complains, and I give her a small, apologetic smile in response. She shakes her head. "People think you kill cops, brother. Now you want to—"

"I don't kill law enforcement members. I police them," I reply tiredly, and take a swallow of my tea. "Carolyn Moss is an asset in mid-acquisition."

"Whom you've got a gigantic crush on." Her expression is still annoyingly amused. In private, she always turns into a little sister, even as she's all business when we're interacting around others. I'm not sure she lets her guard down around anyone but me.

I count to ten internally and shake my head. "It is not a 'crush.' Carolyn Moss simply happens to be attractive, along with having that mix of both maverick and idealist that I find most appealing."

She's giving me a knowing look. I frown and preoccupy myself with my tea.

"Are you gonna meet her face to face?" she presses.

"I haven't decided. It may not be safe for either of us to do so. Daniels has started spying on her more intensively, and I am concerned about a potential confrontation." And the possibility that I might get too attached.

Be honest with yourself, Adrian. You are already too attached, and even Marissa has picked up on it.

"But her boss is pretty much trying to kill her. And for what? Because she won't fuck him?" She leans forward, trying to catch a look at my phone screen. I sip my tea and ignore the attempt, and she finally sits back again, looking irritated. "Seriously, you should just have one of the guys put a bullet in Daniels and be done with it."

I look down at the image of Carolyn again, taken by one of my operatives on her way out of a San Diego hotel. She was half-turned toward the camera when the photo was taken, keeping a careful eye on passing traffic as she walked to her rental car.

In the photograph, her platinum braid shines like new-fallen snow across her shoulder. It's an image from a Romanticist painting: dark, flowing coat; bright scarf; burgundy-rouged lips parted; eyes like jewels.

"I agree that he deserves it, but the situation is too delicate to allow such a ... direct ... solution. He is under close watch by his superiors, and if murdered, they will immediately investigate." I frown and glance out the window. "This will require a subtler approach."

"Any chance he'll fuck up badly enough that his superiors will handle it? Then we can just send somebody into the prison to shank his ass."

I look back at her, considering. "Not likely. His erratic behavior may get him fired, but it will be months before he is properly imprisoned if we let the rusty wheels of the judicial system turn on their own. And he is too dangerous to allow to remain free for that long."

17

"I guess ... I mean, he seems incompetent as hell. The guy's barely covered his tracks, even though he's under a microscope at work. How dangerous could he be?" She's chewing the ice from her glass. I try to ignore the annoying crunching.

"He may be reaching the point where he no longer cares what happens to him. His only real response to stressors is to double down on his misbehavior. He decided to step up his efforts after I punished him by reporting his harassment to his superior—and his wife."

I did it out of anger, and thus impulsively: not my finest hour. Emotions have no place in the administration of justice.

Had I the chance to do it again, I would punish Daniels more directly. I'm more than capable of commissioning a man to manufacture a deadly accident for the assistant director. I simply tried to avoid it too long, and now, it's too late. I can't have him killed; I must ruin him instead.

It's my mistake to correct now. But I must do so in a way that does not expose me, or Carolyn, to further scrutiny by the FBI. Hmm.

Marissa snickers into her hand, dark eyes dancing. "You ratted him out to his wife? That's cold."

"It was thoroughly deserved. He chased his subordinates behind her back while she was recovering from a mastectomy." On that count alone, I would gladly dispose of him.

Her laughter stops and her hand clenches into a fist. "Oh hell, brother. Give me a gun. I'll finish him myself. Scumbag."

"Don't joke about that," I say, sighing gently. "You don't need that mark on your soul. Leave such ugly work to me."

"Don't be so dramatic. You know I'm just kidding." She winks at me and takes a few swallows of tea. "But seriously, he's obviously bad news. The last thing we need is another evil bastard in a position like that."

I snort and go back to looking at my phone. "As I mentioned, I suspect strongly that at this point, Assistant Director Daniels has reached a level of instability and impulsiveness that will only grow over time. That does not bode well for anyone, but it means that he will likely make increasingly obvious mistakes."

Mistakes that I will gleefully exploit. Just as I exploited his lack of a secure password on his work computer before he got marginally better at covering his tracks.

"What are the chances that he'll manage to force her to turn on you, even if she doesn't want to?" She tosses her whole lemon slice into the glass without twisting it.

I chuckle, looking down at the photo of Carolyn again. "That's the most ironic part of all of this. He's already sending her after me. She simply hasn't made the connection yet. And as for Daniels ... he has no idea that she and I have been in contact for months." I give her a softly wicked smile, and her eyebrows rise.

"Okay," she admits, "I'm impressed. I want to see where you're going with this."

"You will," I promise. "Depending on how the endgame goes, I may pull you in on handling some of it."

It's an hour and a half before we touch down—rerouted to DCA, just like Carolyn's commuter plane before us. I have my driver reroute and pick us up, then I sit impatiently in the limousine and sip butterscotch schnapps now and again to keep my palate stimulated. I'm bored to tears without a computer in front of me.

I hate working away from one of my data hubs. I have command centers set up in every major city that I frequent: Baltimore, Detroit, Chicago, New York, DC, Seattle, and a dozen others. More information passes through my systems in one hour than through entire university networks in a week.

The hubs are my seats of power. Once I'm at the keyboard in one of them, I'm directly in the driver's seat of my growing empire.

It's from there that I can head off problems, learn the secrets of enemies and allies alike, and do real good. I have no idea how much new knowledge is waiting for me when we finally land on the doorstep of my mansion outside Baltimore. I'm just glad that I don't have to wait much longer to get back to it all.

The sprawling manor house once belonged to an enemy. The man is long dead—one of the first people in the world who I can take credit for destroying. He preyed on someone I loved, once upon a time, and it led to her death. In return, I ruined him, took everything he had, and drove him to suicide.

Now I walk again into what was once his home, gained by right of conquest, and remade in my image. The entry hall smells faintly of Florida Water, a personal favorite, and of the freshly blooming magnolias that shade the front entrance. I'm glad to be away from dreary New York to someplace where spring has already taken hold.

"I'll be in my lab!" Marissa calls as she bounds ahead of me and down the first-floor hallway. She's been tinkering with a robotics project for the better part of a month, some combination of drone and guard dog. It's not clear yet if she'll continue with this or flit toward some other facet of technology that interests her.

That's all right. She has the gift, and she will learn focus soon enough. She can be young and flighty within the safety of our home. It's one of the reasons that I rescued her: to give her the chance to chase joy as well as purpose.

As for me, I have long since found joy in my purpose, and so most of the time, pursuing the one is pursuing the other.

I make my way down the broad marble steps into the basement section that I walled off and turned into my computer center. Beyond the door, the air is filled with the soft hum of the constantly working machines' cooling fans, mixed with the rumble of the climate control system. I take a bottle of water from the small glass-fronted fridge by the door as I walk in; all the equipment makes the air dry, and I don't want to end up with another sinus headache.

The Baltimore hub is my largest and oldest in the States. Centered on a brand-new, custom-built quantum computing system, it searches, sorts, and prioritizes information and messages with the aid of powerful algorithms that I created myself. Surrounding the black metal column that contains it are a variety of subsystems running in parallel. In front of it stands my broad black desk with its bank of enormous flat screens.

Above the screens, a large-format single-line digital display panel is bolted to the wall. It looms over everything, showing an ever-growing number that is now up to nine digits. Hundreds of millions updated every second by an AI dedicated to monitoring the internet for specific status updates.

Just under the display panel is the legend "successes." As I watch, the number jumps. Five more.

I smile. It's been a good day, looking at the numbers.

I sit down at the main screen and pull the keyboard from a drawer, pressing my thumb to its built-in scanner. The system recognizes me and unlocks; all the screens glow to life and fill up with file directories, flow charts, marked maps, and information webs on a variety of subjects.

I check my email. Carolyn has received my package and is safely tucked away in a room that her superior does not know the number or location of. I don't know if she'll be able to access her old room, but if she does and my suspicions are correct, she'll soon learn the lengths to which Daniels is now going to either implicate her in something or destroy her.

He will not be allowed to succeed.

I check the East Coast section for alerts. None of the subjects being watched have updated information, including Daniels, frustratingly. I know he must be planning something besides pitting her against the demon that he thinks I am. Probably in the hopes that I'll kill her.

In Daniels's current mental state, escalation is his only perceived option. He's not the self-destructive type, at least not consciously or actively. He would be far easier to deal with if he was.

Instead, if I don't conveniently kill Moss for him, he'll likely either call her back for a close-to-home betrayal of some kind or send someone else after her. I have to keep an eye on him and try to predict his next moves, to keep Carolyn safe.

But that does not mean that I am in love with her.

Perhaps I've indulged too much in wishful thinking about her. Perhaps I am too concerned. Perhaps I am too involved—but despite Marissa's teasing, I am still in control of myself.

And so much more than myself. I open my messages to example after example of just how wide my influence has grown.

My operatives have checked in for the day; I scan through dozens of emails containing their latest updates on their current assignments. No real fires to put out; I answer the few questions posed to me and then move on to my assets.

They, unfortunately, are a mess. There's a politician in Iowa begging me for help with a blackmail attempt. There's a new chief of police in the San Francisco Bay Area who has just learned the depths of corruption in his city's police department and is asking for advice. There's a billionaire in south Florida whose wife and baby son have been kidnapped.

I sit back, sighing and rubbing my temples. I want to skip all of it and go back to checking in on Carolyn, but I know that's a bad idea. I must be impartial, I must be thorough, and I must not let anything slide.

My work is too important.

The politician is instructed to stop visiting prostitutes while I take care of his blackmailer. I put one of my men in Iowa on it and move on.

I need more information from the police chief. I put him in contact with a San Francisco member of Internal Affairs for advice on cleaning house and to gather more details on the situation for me.

The billionaire reminds me of my father in his learned helplessness: he flails in the face of the slightest problems despite his ability to spend money to make it all go away. The kidnappers are career professionals who are literally in it for a ransom amount he could pay out of pocket. I tell the billionaire to set up the drop, and then send a man to find and eliminate both kidnappers before they can victimize anyone else.

Perhaps it's harsh, but I've been telling the man to get his wife her own bodyguards for five years. I'll drop the ransom money into her account for a nice fresh start once she divorces him. I hope she takes their son.

From then, it's on to my current cases: ordinary people, communities, and organizations in need of my aid. They form the core of my activities, far more than consolidating my power.

In fact, my growing power is in many ways a means to this end. Some are aware of me and make their requests directly; others, I have learned about from concerned people, news articles, or my assets in various cities.

The requests are endless. Prometheus, help me save my business. Prometheus, help me find my child. Prometheus, a man too rich for the police to stop is stalking me.

Prometheus, a company stole our water supply and we are dying. Prometheus, there is a serial killer loose. Prometheus, my home has been decimated by war.

I do everything I can ... and what I can do is a great deal.

This is how I found Carolyn Moss. Her predicament was clear from the beginning: a young, brilliant idealist caught up in a web of bureaucracy, corruption, and exploitation by her predatory boss. She has no idea just how many bullets I have helped her dodge, though I know she's grateful for what she does know about.

One day, I hope to explain the whole ugly story to her. But if I tell her just how deep Derek Daniels's cruelty, corruption, and vindictiveness goes, she will get even angrier. Extremes of emotion cause one to make mistakes, and she is already in a hazardous position.

It takes me three solid hours of work to clear my most pressing cases and answer all urgent messages. I still have a pile of work to do tweaking the search algorithms and giving commands to my various information-gathering AIs, but I decide to take a break and drink another bottle of water—and then check in on Carolyn.

There are dozens of ways for me to watch over her, from monitoring her emails, texts, and phone calls, to checking CCTV feeds. She's never completely out of my reach ... which means she's never lacking in my protection.

I lean forward and speak into my microphone. "Hermes, locate subject Carolyn Moss."

The AI pops up a response: **Working. Please stand by.** Ten seconds pass. **Located.**

"Please provide any relevant internet-connected camera feeds in the area." I'm calm, collected, and confident that whatever is going on, and however Carolyn receives the news of her boss's latest betrayal, she'll be fine. She's smart, creative, and independent—and she has me to help her.

Then the image feed of the hotel lobby hits my eyes, and I see her sitting on a couch there, wiping tears.

A cold surge of emotion runs through me; it goes far beyond concern, leaving me flooded with adrenaline. I hurriedly set aside my water bottle and reach for my phone.

CHAPTER 3

Carolyn

*W*hat do I know about Prometheus?

Even less than I know about Adrian DuBois, I realize, as I wait for the courier to arrive. He's got a Maryland accent. He's a certified computer genius and seems to have incredible access to information, both online and in the underworld.

He's interested in me. By his own words.

Not to mention that I owe him my life and my continued, if unorthodox, success in my career. If not for him, Daniels would have gotten his way and wrecked things for me before the year started.

The courier shows up, tapping at my door. She's in a typical bike messenger's uniform of bright tech-fabric clothes and black cross-body bag; there's rain in her spiky yellow hair. We barely talk; I sign for the package she offers me, then she takes off.

I stare down at the small box with the anonymous label for a few seconds before finally going to my desk and opening it up. Inside is a small piece of electronics shaped a little like a laser thermometer, but without the laser or trigger. Just an ON switch beside its small, square display.

I turn it on, take one look at the readout, and realize what I'm holding: a high-end transmitter detector. A fucking bug detector. Does he think someone bugged my hotel room? Maybe DuBois?

I turn the little tool over and over in my hand, its weight seeming to get heavier over time. He's never steered me wrong before ... as far as I know, anyway. I need to get a look at that room.

I know something's wrong almost right away when the reception desk finally gets back to me.

The receptionist is a perky young man who sounds like he is early enough in his shift to still have some enthusiasm to spare. The first thing out of his mouth is, "Hi, Special Agent, this is Darren downstairs. I wanted to find out if your luggage has been returned to you? The other FBI agents went through your room before you called me, and I had hoped they would return your stuff."

My heart starts pounding, and nausea creeps up the back of my throat. Other agents?

I need to find out what is going on in that room and I need to do it now. "Um, almost everything, but there was a small item missing that they may have overlooked. Do you mind sending someone over to let me in?" I keep my voice sweet and worried, like any well-mannered hotel guest.

"Oh, of course. I'll just get someone to cover the desk and let you in myself. Five minutes?" I hear him typing.

"Sounds good. I'll meet you outside." I hang up, and then sit there a moment, limbs heavy, trembling.

Why are there other FBI agents here? Is it Daniels's doing, or are the locals checking up on me? Why are they doing anything behind my back?

A sudden, creeping suspicion fills me. Did Daniels find out about Prometheus somehow? Does he think I'm going to go rogue?

I let out a nervous little laugh as I shove the bug detector and room key in my pocket and grab my phone. By bureau standards, I went rogue a long time ago. I ended up driving back from Mexico with a world-class assassin tied up in my trunk.

That's not exactly a legal extradition.

Nor is it by the book to be sharing information with an outlaw hacker whom I know little about. But in return, I've gotten more help in doing my job than I ever have from Daniels.

I make my way down to the fourth floor, determined to sort all of this out and then get back to my investigation. All I have to do is get through this case. It may take me months, and by the time I'm done, Daniels will probably have been sacked and replaced anyway.

I'm surprised that he's made it this long without ending up either out on his butt, in jail, or both. This isn't the 1960s. You can't simply get away with such garbage against female employees because you're the boss. And I have no doubt that he was doing the same thing way before his wife got cancer or I came on the scene.

I step out of the elevator—and freeze. There's a group of men in cheap suits, wearing FBI badges hanging over the edge of their breast pockets, just exiting room 407—the one I told Daniels I'm staying in. I hurriedly step into the alcove for the drinking fountain next to me, holding my breath and praying they don't walk past the elevator and spy me.

I hear them talking as they approach and breathe as quietly as I can.

"So, what did AD Daniels say about her?" He has a Brooklyn accent and my heart immediately sinks.

"Something about potential cooperation with one of her targets. He's worried she'll flip on us."

"Wait. Is this the same girl he was bitching about last week? I looked up her record. She's good. No issues with her work performance, and she brought in fucking Genova last month." This one has the decency to sound impressed.

"That shit doesn't matter. Plenty of good agents end up taking bribes now and again just from how shitty our pay is." I hear the ding of the elevator being summoned, and I shiver, keenly aware that they're steps away from me.

"Yeah, but since when do we go in agents' rooms and—"

"Shut up, Wallace. There's no use complaining about it. Daniels is the AD, he sent us down here to do a job, we did it. Let's go grab a bite to eat and not worry about it."

"Yeah, good idea. I'm starving," a third agent said. "You got any idea why he sent four of us? Armed?"

"No idea, man. Maybe he thinks she's dangerous. Anyway, she just barely got off the damn plane an hour ago. She's probably getting something to eat, too." The second one stifled a yawn.

"Yeah, I'm kinda glad she didn't walk in on us. That would have taken some explaining." The third one laughs, and the others join him as the elevator dings and rattles open.

I hear them step inside and the door close. Then I let out all my breath in a huff. So, it's Daniels. And either he suspects something, or he's preparing to frame me.

All of this because I wouldn't fuck him. How did his wife endure him, if he's this rapey and vindictive? How has he stayed out of jail?

The worst part of all of this isn't discovering that Daniels is even more of a scumbag than I thought. It's the men following his crazy orders with barely a question in their heads.

Maybe I've long since gone rogue.

Or maybe it's the men on Daniels's list. They were universally framed as monsters in his notes. Yet each one has turned out to basically be a good man trying to get out of his criminal lifestyle.

Maybe it's the list that has me questioning everything. Doubting myself, doubting the Bureau, doubting the legal system. It's like Daniels has accidentally walked me through an introduction to just how morally gray most things are even when you think you're one of the good guys.

I keep questioning why he picked these men, just like I question why he sends me everywhere with no backup. The second one I could chalk up to spite, immaturity, and lack of professionalism. But the first one has had me constantly baffled me since the start of this investigation.

I make my way down the hall to room 401. I already know what I'm going to find there, but I'm still bracing myself. There's still this part of me that doesn't want to believe that it's gotten this bad.

I'm standing there for less than a minute when a slim, brown-haired young man in the receptionists' uniform comes out of the elevator and hurries down the hall. He sees me and slows down, smiling a little.

"Hi," he says cheerily. "Did you catch your coworkers?"

"Just missed them," I lie regretfully. "I've just got one tiny bag missing, and it's either going to be in here or in 407."

"Oh, well, that's not a problem," he replies, pulling his keys off his belt. "I'll just open this up and check inside for you."

"Um ... maybe you should let me do it," I venture.

"It's no problem. I don't mind doing a little hunting." He has a cute smile. First job, maybe—trying hard to impress everyone.

That's still not going to work. "It's a tampon bag."

His eyes widen slightly, and he blushes. "Um ... oh. I uh ... okay. How about I wait out here and you look for it? I don't mind opening up the other room, too."

I give him a smile. "Thanks. You're a big help. Make sure to give me your card so I can put in a good word with your boss."

He beams and I struggle to keep the sadness out of my smile. If only my biggest problem was impressing a normal, ordinary, non-predatory boss. Instead, here I am, checking up on Daniels checking up on me, while the one man I wish was here with me is someone I have never met.

I'm not sure what bothers me more: the gnawing loneliness that has gotten so much worse since Prometheus gave me a taste of kindness or the creeping mix of toxic emotions from dealing with Daniels.

The receptionist hands me a card and then lets me in. I nod to him gratefully and hurry into the suite. He shuts the door as if he doesn't even want to see me retrieve the fatal tampon bag.

Yeah, I thought that would work. He's still in his teens, and I know a lot of grown men who are still freaked out by periods and other female bodily functions.

Yet another reason why I've never been on more than a few dates, barely been kissed, and never had sex. I can't stand the idea of making love to a man who can only tolerate my body when it's giving him pleasure—but that seems to mean passing over an awful lot of men.

Life's not fair. I've known that since I was a little girl stuck with my ass of a father. Who was also freaked out by periods.

I turn on the detector and sweep it around the place, listening for the telltale beep that says it's picked up a transmission. Quickly, my heart sinks: there are at least four of them. The bed beeps, the bathroom beeps, the desk beeps, by the phone beeps.

The bathroom, too, huh? Fuck you, Daniels.

I check behind the headboard of the bed and see the small transmitter stuck to its back. It's got a single green LED on the back, blinking every once in a while, like a slow heartbeat. I stare at the thing in my hand and then shake my head and put it back where I found it.

I can't dismantle, disable, or remove them. If I leave them in place, whoever rents the room will have their conversations picked up by the transmitters, and the surveillance team that is probably following me will soon realize that they bugged the wrong room. Rooms.

Plural, because I'm almost sure they also bugged 407.

Which is exactly when Daniels is going to find out that I lied to him about what suite I'm in. I know he already doesn't trust me, because he left the transmitters in 401—in case I lied about moving. He's trying to catch me doing something wrong.

If I don't figure out how to deal with these transmitters, he will catch me, and there's nothing I'll be able to do about it.

I am going to need Prometheus's help with the damned things, with the surveillance team, and with DuBois. I'll owe him big by the end of it, and that just leaves me feeling even more vulnerable.

I wish I knew more about Prometheus before I go connecting myself to him even more deeply with things like debt ... and emotions. It's risky.

And yet ... he's been so kind to me. He always keeps his word and he listens to me. When we spoke on the phone, I felt I could tell him anything ... though, of course, I kept things from getting too personal.

The warm feeling I get thinking about his calls is beautiful and unfamiliar—and leaves me wanting more. He can make a conversation about anything seem more interesting and does it all in a voice so beautiful that it makes me weak.

He makes me weak. He gets in under my guard. He reminds me, tenderly and a little cruelly, that as independent as I am, I am also lonely.

31

"Not in there," I sigh as I come back out. "I know they checked in over at 407, maybe they thought that was the suite I picked? Do you mind if I look in there?"

The receptionist gives me a polite nod, and down the hall we go, while my heart hammers in my ears and despair settles on me like a stone.

What do I do if Daniels succeeds in tarnishing my reputation with the FBI to the point where I spend the rest of my career struggling against it? What if he makes it so hard for me, even on the way out, that I'll end up having to leave? What will I do with myself?

My father, who hated every breath I drew, laughed at me when I said I was joining the FBI. He told me that I would never even manage to graduate, especially since he wasn't paying for a dime of it. I have spent my entire career proving him wrong: graduating from my four-year university with honors, going to Quantico, completing my agent training and my training as a profiler, and then forcing myself to soldier on with my first assignment in spite of what Daniels keeps trying to do.

I want to cry as I smile at the young man, who unlocks the door and lets me into the hotel room where Daniels thinks I'm staying. My heart's in my shoes as I slip inside, pull out the bug detector, and confirm, once again, that Daniels is attempting to perform surveillance on me for the duration of my stay. Which he knows could be months.

And he got some of my fellow agents to go along with it.

A terrible sense of isolation runs through me when the bug detector softly beeps. I know now that I can't trust the Bureau anymore.

That just leaves one person who I can.

I come back out with a bright smile pasted on. "Thanks so much. I found it." I pat my pocket and he nods. I hand him a tip. He hands me a card and we part company.

Only when he's out of sight do I let myself lean against the wall and curse under my breath. I've fought depression my whole life thanks to my father, pitting everything from mental training to medication to nutrition to sheer will against the creeping sense that nothing will ever go right no matter how hard I fight to achieve my goals.

My father believed that of me. The depression wants me to believe it. And now, Daniels may be making it happen.

These thoughts boil in my head, leaving me agitated and on the verge of tears. The despair keeps pressing down on me harder and harder, trying to smother my resolve.

Keep moving, I tell myself. Prometheus may be able to help, but you've still got to do the work.

I go back upstairs to my suite, intent on distracting myself with paperwork and research for the case. From what I've been able to tell so far, DuBois's primary business in town is an elegant, 1940s-style nightclub in downtown Baltimore. He can be found at his personal table most Saturday nights when he's in town. The best thing I can do to connect with him is to seek him out there.

That means getting a nice outfit. Daniels, the cheap bastard, will probably balk at approving reimbursement for it, which means I'll have to dry clean it and return it—or get something I like enough that I might wear it a second time for a different occasion.

At least shopping will get my mind off ... all of this.

That's it. I'll leave a message with Prometheus, go get a nice meal and a nice dress, put in my report with Daniels, and then get some sleep. I just ... wish I wasn't doing all of it alone.

I'm used to isolation. I'm at my most confident and decisive when I'm alone. It's one of the reasons I didn't complain more when I wasn't assigned a field partner.

But loneliness ... loneliness is not something you get used to, any more than being hungry or being tired. There's a part of you that craves the fulfillment of good company, friendship ... love. Being without it won't kill you ... but it never stops gnawing at you either.

My voice shakes annoyingly as I leave a short message for Prometheus.

"Hi. I know you won't get this until later, but ... I got your gift, and I found what you figured I would. I don't know what to do to handle this kind of technology, so if you could give me a call with some pointers when you're free, I'd appreciate it.

"Thank you again for everything," I say softly, with warmth in my voice that sounds a bit more than professional. I can't help that.

I change my clothes into jeans and a royal blue blouse, put on a windbreaker, and cover my hair with a bright scarf. I know the platinum blonde braid is my most distinctive feature, and I don't feel like having it wave like a flag behind me as I go out on errands.

When I get downstairs, it has warmed up, but it's still raining. I'm so glad it isn't snow and ice, so I don't mind. But my thoughts are still chasing me, threatening to weigh my heart down with despair.

Of course, there's a white delivery van parked in the space next to my rental car, which probably has a LoJack on it now. I don't want to deal with any of that. I walk instead, shouldering my way through the warm rain.

I eat fried chicken at a diner four blocks down, and then look up boutiques online and have an Uber take me into the shopping district.

It takes me a while to find an elegant gown that both flatters me and fits within my laughable budget. I finally settle on a deep blue gown which makes my skin and hair look even paler and my eyes brighter. It's sleeveless, simple, Grecian, and goes with the gold-and-burgundy scarf and gold flats that I bought.

I never, ever wear heels on the job. I can wear a slinky dress and strap my gun to my inner thigh but running and fighting in heels is far less efficient than it's portrayed in the movies. Kicking them off and running barefoot is faster and less likely to result in a fall, but it's still not ideal.

When I get back to the hotel, the van is still sitting next to my car. I walk inside—and almost immediately, my phone rings. This time I check it—and frown. Daniels again.

I pick up. "I've reached the hotel."

"Where were you? I thought you had checked in." He sounds confused, angry. He's probably wondering why the bugs haven't picked up anything yet.

"Food and supplies," I explain patiently. "Plus, I have a lead on where DuBois will be Saturday. I'm going to be there."

"Hmm. Well, I guess I can't be too pissed if you were out chasing leads. Put everything you've got in your report and remember to log your mileage."

He already sounds suspicious, grudging. Or does he always sound this way? What does he suspect? Does he know about Prometheus?

No. I've been careful about that. "Of course. Is there anything else?"

"Yeah. I want you calling in twice a day now—start and end of shift. Log your locations and times." He hangs up, and I stare at the phone, shivering slightly.

He's going to have me tracked so he can see if I'm lying about where I go. That bastard. Fortunately, he's not nearly as subtle as he thinks he is.

But as what Daniels is doing overwhelms me, the depression comes flooding back. Watching me, restricting me, laying traps. Turning up the pressure every day, every hour, until he either catches me in something illegal or I quit.

He must want me to quit. Prometheus worries that there's more to it than that, but that's enough to scare me.

I sit down on one of the benches in the lobby, my head pounding and my eyes stinging. I take off my scarf and use it to dab at my cheeks. Crap.

If he forces me to quit and I cave in, he'll be proving my father right. He'll be proving the depression my father left me with right. I can't cave in. But this ... this is agonizing.

I'm wiping tears of frustration from my eyes when my phone rings again. I check it. It's Prometheus.

I let out a little sob of relief.

CHAPTER 4

Carolyn

*T*he first thing out of Prometheus when I answer his phone call is, "Are you all right?"

I wipe my eyes self-consciously, even though he can't see me. "I'm trying to be."

"What happened?" I can hear the concern in his voice. It's bizarre. We've never met. He's refused to meet me, in fact. Why is he worried?

"Well, uh ... I should get upstairs. I'm in the lobby." I manage to stand and head for the elevator, not wanting to discuss my private feelings or any of my needs where others might overhear. "Did you get my message?"

"Yes, I did." He sounds distracted suddenly. I hear him take a swallow of something. "I can assist. Go upstairs and call me back."

My mood lightens as I go back to my room. The change is so sudden that I have to lean against the elevator wall. It's like a tremendous pressure has been lifted off me.

I am no longer alone. Except physically, of course. But the single life-line of Prometheus's phone call is enough to help me bounce back.

I'm tough, but I have my limits. It's nothing to be ashamed of to have them, no matter what my father thought. But I still feel a lot better about myself when my eyes stop leaking and the trembling stops.

I'm still an FBI agent, and a better cop, investigator, and person than my father ever was. I'm not going to let his predictions come true, and I'm not going to let Daniels push me out of my job.

I just don't know how I'm going to win out yet. But I've fought my way this far—I can keep fighting. And at least I have one person I can rely on.

Back in my room, I find myself overcome by a sudden wave of suspicion. I was gone for hours. What if the agents found out what room I moved to already?

What if they talked their way into this room, too, went through my things, and left transmitters behind?

Everything seems to be where I left it, but these guys are professionals. We're trained on how to search a room without leaving any trace that we've been there. All they would have to do is take a few photographs of how the room looked beforehand and then put it back that way after the search.

I pull out the bug detector and sweep every room. Not a single beep. Thank God. One less thing to worry about. I sit down on the bed to call Prometheus back.

When he picks up, he sounds a little tired, as if today has also been a struggle for him. "Are you back in your room?"

I set aside the bug detector on the nightstand. "Yeah. I ... thank you for calling." It's needless—I asked him to. But I'm still pathetically grateful.

What is it about this man? Is it his mystery, his brilliance, or his kindness toward me? I don't even know what he looks like, let alone how he lives his life or if he's even dating or married to someone.

I shouldn't be falling for him. But here we are.

"Of course. So, you discovered the transmitters."

"Yes. I'm facing a catch-22 as a result, Prometheus. If I tamper with the transmitters, he'll know. If I leave them be, he'll soon learn that I lied about what room I was in." I'm certain Daniels deliberately set things up this way.

"Mm, yes. You're going to need to do something that he hasn't planned for." I hear a faint tapping sound and a sip.

"Like what?" I'm dizzy and tired; I've been dealing with all of this too long. I need that damn nap.

"Confront him." His voice is smooth with self-assurance.

Wait, what? "Prometheus, that sounds like kicking a hornet's nest."

"Oh, it is, and he may retaliate, but doing so will avoid his attempts to entrap you." He starts typing. "The best he can do right now within the scope of his legal powers is to harass you and put you at risk. Catching him in something completely outside of the law gives you leverage, and he'll know it. With all the scrutiny he's under, he'll quickly be in serious trouble for something like, say, illegal surveillance and misusing bureau resources."

"Why not just go to his superior?" My heart's beating faster, but with excitement, not fear. Why didn't I think of all this?

"You can, if you wish, but the threat may be enough to make him back down." He mutters something under his breath that I don't catch.

"Reporting him without the warning may well just make him even more irrationally angry, and he's already antagonizing you."

"Okay, I'll keep that in mind." I'm going to compose a letter to his boss with everything I know so far and decide whether I'm sending it after talking to Daniels. "What about the surveillance team?"

"I would be equally frank with them." Sip. "Of course, they're simply doing the work assigned to them by a corrupt superior. You should probably keep that in mind."

"Oh, I will." Once I get a break. Otherwise, I might be short with them. "Thank you."

"Is there anything else? You seem upset." There's that concern again, warming me all through.

"Dealing with some personal issues," I mumble, cheeks prickling with embarrassment. "This mess with Daniels has brought them to mind. It's nothing to be concerned about."

"I'm still concerned." His voice is soft. "I'm afraid it can't be helped."

Oh no. Don't do that. It makes me want things that I can't have, and that hurts. "I still wish you would let me meet you," I murmur.

There's a long silence, worrying me. But then he shocks me pleasantly by saying, "I'll ... consider it."

My heart lifts as he says that. I never expected he would take me up on my request after what happened in Detroit. "Please do. It has nothing to do with work. It's personal."

At once, I get nervous, as I never expected to admit to him that I'm starting to have feelings for him. Have I said too much? Am I just leaving myself open to manipulation?

No doubt about it—I am. Attraction makes one vulnerable. He could use my confession against me.

"I know," he says in an almost tender tone. There's something like wistfulness in his voice, and my heart starts beating even faster. "I

40

would not visit you for business, Carolyn. I would visit because I find you intriguing."

I'm trembling again, but it's not because I'm upset. Instead, I'm brimming over with a mixture of quiet joy and a strange excitement. What does he mean by "intriguing"?

Is he referring to me personally, or is this a seduction? After all, I already know that seduction is a common way of swaying someone to your side. I don't know enough about Prometheus to figure out if that's something that he would do to me.

"I can't stop thinking about you, either." The hushed confession pours out of me before I can stop it.

That was stupid. I have now doubled down on making myself vulnerable to him, and I know already that any intelligent criminal would consider me a valuable asset. I am, after all, a law enforcement officer who is already cooperating with him more than I strictly should.

He could be playing me.

But I have to believe in someone besides myself. Right now, the people who should be the good guys are the ones who I have to watch out for. With the exception of DuBois, of course. He's still on my to-do list—if only to keep up appearances.

But first, I have to deal with the damn FBI surveillance. And then, I have to deal with my feelings for Prometheus. After that, I can go put on my slinky new dress, and maybe convince this mysterious crime lord that I want to come work for him.

Or maybe, I'll just have a nice night out at his club, log my "work," and string Daniels along some more while I figure out what to do.

When it comes to dealing with my feelings for Prometheus, I'm drawing a big blank. If I get to see him, maybe I'll be able to work everything out. Maybe I can either break the spell by discovering that I'm not physically attracted to him, or maybe ...

Maybe something will happen between us. That thought leaves me breathless.

"I understand," he finally says. His voice still has that tender note that I never expected. "But there is significant risk involved in our associating directly, for both of us. I must weigh these risks against my real desire to get to know you better."

Oh God. My knees squeeze together, and I have trouble catching my breath. He wasn't just talking about face-to-face conversation. That is clear.

"I get it," I quickly stammer. "I ... should change the subject."

"Perhaps you should," he replies kindly and with a little regret.

Okay, time for the third thing on my list. I don't know how I'm toughing through this intense conversation, but I need to at least mention why I came to Baltimore in the first place.

"I still need to do my job," I admit. "Do you mind?"

"My time is yours," he purrs, and my toes curl inside my rain boots.

"I—I—" Get it together, Carolyn. "I need assistance figuring out how to best get close to Adrian DuBois."

There is a long silence, and for a moment, I worry I've finally overstepped my bounds somehow. But this conversation has been full of those kinds of moments, and each time, things have come out all right. I brace myself, hoping that I haven't ruined the mood.

"I see," he finally muses. "You realize that it will be impossible to bring Adrian DuBois in."

"It isn't about that," I insist. "You see, this list of men that I was given by Daniels to chase over the winter have all been... that is, they have all somehow led to other people who deserved to be brought in even more. You have encouraged me to pursue these alternate suspects, and except for the one who died, every last one of them is in prison or headed that way.

"If I had brought in any of the men I was actually after, chances are that no real case could have been built against them. Their records are so thin and the evidence against them so weak and circumstantial, I would have had to catch them actually in the act of shooting someone to be able to make any charges stick." My frustration with being assigned to them boils over suddenly inside me; I keep my voice reasonably professional, but I feel like screaming.

"I see." More silence, giving me a moment to catch my breath. "Go on."

"The evidence against Adrian DuBois is paper-thin no matter how scary the rumors about him are. I understand this. I also understand that he is so powerful, he will likely never see the inside of prison. But I'm under a microscope right now. I am expected to turn in a work log twice a day, and if I make no move toward DuBois, Daniels will know.

"It's another catch-22. I can either chase a guy I don't have a prayer against, or I can give up my job." And it shouldn't be like this.

"I see. So, you are concerned about your work status as a young FBI agent."

"Yes. I believe that Daniels is trying to drive me out of the FBI. I can't yet prove any worse intentions than that." Not to mention his immaturity and spite, more even than my father.

I hear him sip something again and start to wish I had a bottle of water. "I can," he mutters. "There is certain information that has come into my possession that you should be made aware of. I will gather all of it and contact you soon with every bit. But suffice it to say the Daniels is not simply attempting to harass you out of your job. He has much more lethal intentions."

That makes me nervous all over again. What the hell is Daniels planning? "Is there anything besides the surveillance that I should be immediately concerned about?"

"These are things you should keep in mind regularly when dealing with him. I will continue to monitor him, so if there is a spike in his activities, I should be able to let you know. Daniels will do what he can to remove you from his department and his presence. In addition, he wants revenge for his wounded pride. You have likely already noticed that he has broken protocol several times simply to make your work harder. He apparently believes that because you are an inexperienced agent, you wouldn't notice.

"Of course, this is incorrect. You are brilliant and resourceful, and despite him giving you a list of essentially impossible tasks, you have still managed to make solid arrests of related individuals. But I am afraid that this has simply angered him further." His tone hovers somewhere between regret and disdain.

Finally, I voice my real worries. "Prometheus, I'm not certain that will be good enough for the FBI. After all, Daniels set me up to fail. All they are going to see in my work reports is that I didn't bring in the suspect I was assigned to."

His keyboard clicks rapidly. "I don't think that your professionalism will be called into question by anyone else at the FBI, most especially his superiors. They are now aware of Daniels's corruption, if not of the lengths to which he will go to get what he wants. Unfortunately, like yourself, they have not yet seen everything he has done or tried to do. I have seen most of it, as I have been monitoring him since before you and I even communicated." He takes a bigger gulp of his drink.

My mouth goes dry. "Maybe you should just tell me everything now."

"I will present that evidence to you as soon as I have it all available. But I assure you, Daniels is likely to escalate dangerously. You have had too much success in spite of him, and he's not happy about it. I'm sorry to be so blunt, but Derek Daniels is pitting you against DuBois specifically because he believes the man will have you killed for interfering in his business."

"How do you know all of this?" I can't imagine what kind of resources and hacking skills he must have to be able to keep this close watch on Daniels—or on me for that matter. It's a little scary.

But it must be much, much scarier for those on Prometheus's bad side. People like Daniels. I can at least take comfort in that.

"After discovering that Daniels was looking for a specific set of men for you to chase, which included the employee of a business associate, I was alerted to his plans and began monitoring him. It's safer for you if I don't divulge my methods." He sounds warm and calm, as if supremely confident that he can protect me from Daniels and everything else.

I find myself wishing that was true. "So, are you suggesting I stay away from DuBois even though I'm supposed to be going to his club on Saturday night?"

There's a pause. Then, almost eagerly, he states, "No, by all means, come to the club. You said Saturday?"

"Yes." He's being mysterious again. It only makes me more curious. "Is there something special about Saturday besides him being there?"

"No, not in particular. I simply wanted the timeframe so I could check up on your situation more precisely." More typing. "I will get you what information I can about DuBois, but remember: you won't be able to take him in. It's a lost cause." He sounds more apologetic than anything else.

"Do you think he would kill me?" Daniels has been absolutely wrong about every other guy on the list, but what about a billionaire reputed crime lord?

He chuckles softly for some reason. "No. But he will know who and what you are. Is there anything else, Carolyn?"

I want him to know those things if I decide to go through with investigating him. My whole premise is that I'm a burned-out FBI agent looking for a better opportunity. The last thing I want is for someone like DuBois to catch me in a lie.

Though right now, I have to lie to Prometheus, which fills me with regret. The "anything else" is that I just want to keep talking to him, but I've been schoolgirlish enough for one conversation. I need to let go and go do my work.

I force it out. "No, I'm fine now. You've been thorough. Thank you for everything. I will take care of my end of things."

"It has been my pleasure, Carolyn. Please try to get some rest."

I'm trembling a little as I hang up. Giddy. Smiling too much. He flirted with me.

He wants to see me and is only held back by safety issues. Maybe …

I push the thought away, delightful as it is. I need to thwart my vindictive boss and chase a mysterious criminal mastermind. Fantasizing about sleeping with a man I've never even laid eyes on will have to wait.

CHAPTER 5

Adrian

I need a cognac.

What were you thinking, Adrian? I ask myself, getting up from my computer desk and stomping upstairs to visit my wet bar. Why did you admit to Carolyn that you're personally interested in her? Why did you flirt?

Have you completely lost all sense of caution? It's too dangerous to get involved with an FBI agent. The best that can be expected is a cordial business relationship. Not sex—and certainly not romance!

I don't normally drink anything stronger than the cordials I habitually savor in tiny amounts throughout the day, largely for their flavor. I will also have a glass of wine with my dinner. But when under enough strain, I find myself gravitating toward stronger stuff.

The last time I did so was after a lover's funeral. And so, my urge to drink is a red flag all by itself. Just like saying too much to Carolyn.

But the lovely girl just essentially confessed that she's fallen for me. I wonder how terribly lonely she must be that she has done so, even sight unseen, with little idea of who I am when I am not with her. At least I have her delicate, dolphin-eyed beauty to excuse myself with.

Marissa's going to laugh long and loud about this once she gets wind of how this has knocked me off balance. I hate vulnerability. It's embarrassing to discover that this woman has slipped through my armor so easily and has gotten so close to my heart.

Especially when it's too comfortable for me to want her to stop.

But she must. My life is dangerous and full of secrets. She deserves a life in the sun.

In addition, I must always consider the thin blue line that separates us as firmly as a country border. I live outside the law, where I can do the work that benefits humanity most. She upholds the law—however flawed or poorly applied it is.

As I pour two fingers of cognac into my crystal glass, I muse over the possibility of luring Carolyn away from the FBI altogether. If what she wants is to serve the greater good, she can do a great deal more of that with me instead of within the confines of law enforcement.

But when I'm honest with myself, I have to admit it: All I'm doing is making excuses for wanting her with me.

We've never even interacted in person. I'm not sure how this happened. Perhaps it's simply because the two of us are on the same level in many ways.

Like myself, she's an idealist. Like myself, she's that way in part as a reaction against a ... non ideal family life. Unlike myself, she has chosen to work within the system. But I have already seen how ready she is to abandon the protocols of her job in favor of what works better.

I can sympathize with her struggle. I went through a version of it myself, considering various legitimate ventures before finding my path outside the law.

When I was first starting out, I spent a lot of time considering how I could best use my formidable skills and intellect to contribute to humanity. I considered a medical doctorate. I considered technological advances.

Neither of those were sufficient for my purposes. Law enforcement, religious devotion, politics, education—none of them were sufficient. None of them allowed me a wide enough reach that I could influence the lives of people the world over who would not be able to go on without help.

Then one day, entirely by accident, I realized what the solution was. Widespread influence and direct intervention using the only medium capable of reaching the majority of humans on earth: the internet.

Some men in my financial position collect businesses. Some collect real estate. Some collect politicians and celebrities, manipulating their entire careers for their benefit and entertainment.

In my case, after growing considerable wealth from a variety of patents and wise investments, I started expanding my influence not only online but in the underworld. I started collecting and controlling as many non-aligned criminal enterprises as possible. I destroyed many of them, such as rings devoted to human trafficking and child pornography.

Destroying them involved more than destroying their output and freeing the victims. I also destroyed the people involved, those who had profited and satisfied themselves on the suffering of others. As for those who had suffered, I did whatever I could to make sure they were returned to their families, and were given whatever was needed to help get them back on their feet.

It was not just about expanding control. The control was borne out of my need to dispense justice, whether social, financial, or moral. It has never been an end in itself.

As I stand in my library sipping my cognac and staring into the flames of the small fireplace, I wonder how I can possibly explain all of this to Carolyn. I wonder if she could ever accept the reality of the situation and of my life—if she could accept me, not only as her lover, but as the man calling the shots.

I do have a great deal to tempt her with. In return for her loyalty, I could give her a very good life.

My wealth continues to grow despite my considerable expenditures. My power continues to grow despite my regular exercise of it—or perhaps, because of that. Once one has amassed a certain amount of power and wealth and applied them correctly, they tend to increase on their own.

If I could convince Carolyn to come to my side and to serve my vision of a better world, then there would be nothing further to keep us apart. Would she support the idea of a world under my growing, subtle, and secret governance? Would she work with and under me, in the service of a higher and more appropriately applied justice?

I have brought down kings and captains of industry who sowed misery and decay wherever they went. I have stopped wars with a single hack—or a single well-aimed bullet. I have saved entire communities by writing a check.

Would she love me, knowing this? Would she submit to me? Or would she flee?

I realize that I've only taken a few small sips of the cognac. That's a hopeful sign.

Carolyn, what will it take to make you believe in the new order that I would create in the world? I control the powerful. I serve those whom they would prey upon.

More and more each year, Carolyn. I can show you.

I look down at the glass, then go back over to the wet bar and reopen the bottle of cognac. I carefully pour all but perhaps half an ounce back. I don't need its "help," but it does taste quite lovely.

I learned how brutal the world is at ten years old, after my father's cruelty drove my mother to suicide. He never suffered for it until I made him suffer. That is the truth of the world.

We cannot rely on politicians or police, on religious or social institutions, or even on God to give us justice. Current justice systems were made for a world that no longer exists. It has grown beyond them, gotten both darker and more complicated.

Power and wealth are most often used as shields from the consequences of wrongdoing. Even those who are not corrupt are only human and struggle under the weight of a legal system as unevenly applied as it is antiquated. I cannot take law books seriously that still have anti-witchcraft statutes.

I go around the legal system in favor of true justice. Time and again, I see judges and law enforcement officers make the wrong call simply because they are not in full possession of the facts. But with my knowledge aggregators working full-time to distinguish all provable bits of information about any given subject or person, I can have the facts.

The half-open door creaks ajar a little further. I look up and see my sister leaning in the doorway, arms folded, a worried pout on her face. She's still wearing her magnifying goggles on her forehead. I wonder how long she has been working on her robotics project.

"You've got real booze in your hand," she observes. "You all right?"

"I am now," I reassure her calmly. "I'm having half a shot." I knew this was going to happen, but I can't be angry that she's concerned. I know it comes from a good place.

She glances at my glass and nods. "Okay, just checking. That's ... still more than your usual zero, though. It's the FBI agent, isn't it?"

For a moment, it's tempting to deny it. But my sister is one of the few people in my life who can truly keep up with me intellectually, and she will know. "Yes."

"You should go to her," she says gently instead of making fun. I blink at her in surprise, and she shakes her head. "It's obvious that you're stuck on her. You may as well make her face your lock screen, you look at her picture so much. And now you're drinking? Maybe only a little, but still. If it's a two-way thing, don't pass it up. I don't care if she's FBI—you'll find a way of dealing with that. You always do." She walks over, smiling a little.

I consider her, and then set my glass down on the wet bar. "Perhaps you're right."

It will be something of a risk to propose such a thing to Carolyn, but ... I have faced risks before. And she's worth it.

CHAPTER 6

Carolyn

I can't quite deal with the phone call to Daniels yet. I'm too wrung out, and I don't want the little glow from talking to Prometheus again to go away yet. Confronting Daniels is going to be excruciating. It will blow all these good feelings away like a sudden cold wind.

Things are still looking up. My mood's so much better after talking to my strangely attractive mystery hacker that I quickly figure out how to deal with the team of four New York FBI agents sitting in the van downstairs.

This isn't their fault. They didn't even sound happy to be here doing this when I eavesdropped on them. They have their doubts.

So, it's time to approach them like fellow agents, fill them in on the situation, and politely clarify things. Because I'm probably going to need their help.

It's possible that this is a mistake. Maybe Daniels handpicked the biggest sexist assholes he could find to make sure that they'll side with him. But that wasn't what I heard coming out of their mouths.

Some men in my life were and are terrible, like Daniels or my father. But most of them, like many of my colleagues, are completely normal people whose lives and concerns are ninety-five percent similar to my own. Maybe the ones downstairs will be reasonable.

The temperature's still wonderfully above freezing when I venture back out with four room-service mochas under my umbrella with me. I know that this is going to be awkward for all of us—especially them. But I figure that a warm, caffeinated peace offering will help to ease tensions.

Instead of going to my car with the cardboard coffee tray, I go around to the other side of the van and knock politely on the big sliding door. There's a rustle inside and a brief argument that gets a little heated before settling down. I wait patiently, and after a few more moments, the door opens.

They're young—all of them—like me. I recognize one guy, the gawky redhead, from Quantico. They're all smiling a little awkwardly back at me, knowing they're caught and not sure what to say about it.

"Hi, guys. Uh, just for next time's sake, you parked a little close. Try one of the corners or the far end of the lot next time you're watching someone." I smile then and hold out my peace offerings.

"Oh hey." One of them, with dark hair and almost liquid-looking brown eyes, sits forward eagerly to take one. "Thanks. Look, I'm sorry. We just ... uh ..."

"How about we go in under the awning? Everyone's pretty much in for dinner right now." The cramped interior of the van isn't big enough for four tall men and all their surveillance equipment. "I'm not sure there's even room for me in there without the help of a shoehorn."

The first thing I tell them when we get under the shelter of the hotel awning is, "Look, I'm not mad. You're just doing what Daniels told you to do, okay? I know how it goes. That's why I'm in Baltimore, too."

The redhead—Davis, that's his name—shifts uncomfortably and takes a swallow of his mocha before speaking up in a gravelly voice. "There's a whole lot weird about all of this. And I heard a few rumors that Daniels is in some hot water. So how about you tell us what's going on from your perspective?"

"That's fair." I take a deep breath. "Well, Daniels is in hot water because he's been trying to get every woman in the office who's under forty to sleep with him. Including me."

Jaws drop. One guy huffs indignantly, and the brown-eyed one looks embarrassed.

"Shit," Davis mutters, shoving his free hand deep into his trouser pocket. "That sucks. So how does that tie with why we're here?"

"I'm here on a job. He's been sending me after a bunch of suspects all over the country, and the latest is DuBois." I say the last bit flatly.

"Daniels sent you up against Adrian DuBois alone?" Brown Eyes demands. Now they're all staring at me.

"Yes, yes he did. He also didn't assign me a partner, backup, or connections with local law enforcement ... this has pretty much been what he does since I landed in his department and refused to sleep with him." I sigh. "Ask the other women around the office. I'm sure it's why his secretary quit."

"Crap," Brown Eyes grumbles. "So, he sends you out after DuBois alone and has us bug your hotel room and follow you around to make sure you go through with it."

"Yeah, that's pretty much it." I sigh. "And the worst part of all of it is, he's decided to get other agents involved in making my life hard, instead of, say, sending me backup."

"Okay. So ... this is pretty screwed up." Davis sighs. "We can't exactly openly surveil you, but if we go to Daniels now, you know he'll blame us."

"Not if I don't mention you. I was going to talk to him about finding the damn transmitters. I already did, after all." I watch their expressions go from sympathetic and mildly skeptical to guilty as hell in a split second.

"Sorry about that," Davis mutters. "Those were his orders."

"Yeah, well, I'm not using that damn room, so if you guys want to go up to 407 and sleep in a real bed, it's still on his dime. I moved. I don't want that creep listening to me pee." I look appropriately disgusted, though my reasons are far more complicated than that.

"He did make us bug the damn bathrooms," the third one, a blond, says incredulously. The others look even more uncomfortable.

They glance at each other. Davis shrugs. "Okay," he says. "But what do we do now? We can't continue with the surveillance, and we can't just let him send you after DuBois alone. He'll mail your severed head back to Daniels in a box or something."

I frown. I've dug through a lot of scary rumors about DuBois in the last month while preparing for this assignment. Some of them might actually have some truth to them—but I trust Prometheus's assessment more than the rumors.

"I'll figure out how to handle the DuBois thing, and I'm not doing anything recklessly. Yes, Daniels is risking my neck with his bad decisions and lack of support. One day, I might ask you to be witnesses to that fact. But I'm sure not planning to die from it.

"I don't want you on the hook for any decisions I make. I'm going to talk to Daniels about why he's trying to surveil me instead of just handing me a partner as is usual." I hope my smile is reassuring. "If he has any brains, he'll recall you before I get to talking to his boss. Otherwise, I guess we'll talk again."

I look around to see them nodding, all soberly. "Enjoy your mochas, guys, and come in out of the rain. I'm seriously not doing anything more tonight besides yelling at Daniels and sleeping."

A little ripple of laughter goes through them, and we troop inside— them on their way to the reception desk, me back to the elevators and my room.

Well, that went all right. But now, it's time for a showdown.

"Fuck. I'm not looking forward to this." I thump the back of my head against the mirrored elevator wall and try to gather my wits.

You can only afford to tell this bastard about twenty percent of what you want to and stay remotely within the bounds of being professional. Keep it in mind. Do not lose your temper.

"Yeah, easier said than done." I sigh as the elevator stops at my floor. A young couple with matching blue hair passes by in the hallway, drunk and laughing, headed for their room. They're overeager; his hand is already on her breast.

I carefully avoid looking their way again as I walk to my door, swipe my card, and go inside. It's quiet in the room, except for the increasingly aggressive rattle of the rain. I hope the guys took that open hotel room. I also hope they got rid of the transmitters in 401 or shut off that part of the feed.

"Time for the nightly report." I sit at my desk, not wanting to associate lying on my bed with Daniels's impending meltdown. "Here we go."

I call Daniels up and wait. When he picks up, he's yawning, and I quickly realize that he's been drinking. Oh great. This will be even more fun than I thought it would.

"Well, this is a surprise. You actually followed orders and reported in." His voice drips with disdain, forcing me to focus on keeping calm.

Prick. "I always do. At least when it comes to my actual work. Have I ever given you any other impression?"

57

He huffs and snorts angrily. "You know what I mean, you frigid little—"

All right, I'm stopping this right now. "Sir, I just need to ask you one question before we proceed with my report."

That startles him out of his usual train of thought, which was about to lead our conversation right into the gutter—and an argument that I can't afford. "Huh? Fine. Go on."

"Why did you place a surveillance team on me?"

He goes very quiet. Unlike Prometheus's thoughtful silences, this one is full of tension. It's not a matter of me worrying; I can hear his tight, fast breathing.

Well, that shut you up. "Sir, I found multiple listening devices in my hotel room, including in the bathroom." Slight emphasis on that last word.

"Someone bugged the hotel rooms?" he manages, suddenly sounding a lot more sober—and a lot less snide.

Yes, because you ordered them to, you rat. If Prometheus hadn't intercepted that communication, I would have had no idea. And then you would know about the two of us—and that can't happen.

I'm angry enough that the very personal way I'm taking that detail barely registers in my head. My voice, however, stays amazingly calm. "Sir, I've already confirmed that these devices are FBI issue."

He sucks air and briefly fumbles his phone. "Oh, did you?"

The tiny, high note of panic in his voice does me more good than I expected; I actually calm down a little.

Time to play a game of "let's see what the bastard gives away when he's emotionally off-balance."

"Are you aware of the placement of these devices, sir? The four microphone receivers? The camera aimed at the shower?"

"What camera?" he squawks defensively. "I didn't order the placement of any camera—"

That's your second giant Freudian slip in under five minutes. "Sorry, sir?"

"I ... uh ..." He hesitates. "Look, this wasn't my call. You've been under suspicion of being dirty for over a month. It's the whole situation with Assante."

"It wasn't your call? So, you're telling me that the section director ordered my hotel room be bugged and that a camera be placed on my shower stall?" Just keep digging yourself deeper, you complete clown.

"Yes," he snaps finally. "Any orders to bug your room with any devices came from above." He's being deliberately vague, but he has already said too much.

There is a wide, predatory smile on my face now. "So, I should ask the section director why my room was bugged? And about the camera?"

"No, no! Do not go over my head on this. I will handle everything. I'll CC you on the reply. Just hold tight." His voice is shaking. He knows I have him dead to rights; misuse of federal resources gets taken a lot more seriously than trying to screw your subordinates. One word to his boss and his career really will tank.

How many federal laws did you just violate by bugging my room? How much additional trouble are you going to be in when your boss discovers what you have done? I want to laugh at him, but instead I make myself sound concerned.

"Sir, it's your call on how to handle administration, but I'm moving rooms." I even manage to make myself sound a little shaken up. "The violation of my privacy is making it difficult for me to focus on my work."

"Of course, of course. Perfectly understandable. Just contact me with your new room number." He still sounds very nervous.

"I will once I have it." Not a chance, asshole.

I take a deep breath, knowing he's not going to say a damn thing to the section director about this. But that's all right. I don't actually need him to.

Instead I twist the knife just a little.

"Sir, I would appreciate it if you would pass along a comment on my behalf. If the section director has concerns about my professional ethics, there is a system of protocols in place for addressing that. It does not at any point involve placing listening devices in my hotel room, including the bathroom, or filming me in the shower."

And that is when he breaks. "I never told those damn agents to put a camera in the bathroom!"

"Sorry, sir. I didn't quite catch that. Could you say it again?" My chest hitches with repressed laughter.

He knows right away that it's over. He does not yet know that I have witnesses, and that it's too late to manipulate them into silence. But he knows what he just admitted to me, and that it can be proven.

When he sloppily hangs up the phone, my first real laugh of the day bursts out of my mouth and rings off the walls. Got you, you absolute scumbag. Let's see you slime your way out of this one.

Prometheus will be proud of me.

CHAPTER 7

Intermission

Derek

"That absolute bitch!" I sweep half the contents of my desk onto the floor without even thinking about it; my coffee mug goes with it, shattering as it hits and splattering its contents over the fallen paperwork.

I stare at the mess mutely, disgust mixing with my rage. Look at what that woman made me do.

That's it. I'm done. It's been months of dealing with Agent Moss's arrogance and frigidity, even putting up with her trying to rat me out to my superiors for some fake-ass feminist bullshit excuse for an offense.

A man has needs. She's my subordinate. If she's not willing to put out, she gets what she deserves.

Now, she's not only made trouble for me—she's started talking back. I'm no longer willing to wait on her making a misstep with DuBois and getting killed. I want her taken out now.

Fortunately, I've got a plan B.

In the course of chasing all the men who should have killed her, Miss Moss has made herself an enemy even more dangerous than me. Nobody in the Bureau or at the Tombs, where he's being held, believed him when he claimed that Moss made him into a duct-tape mummy and kidnapped him from Mexico to bring him in, but I do.

The bitch is just that crazy.

Anyway, as I phone for the janitor on duty to come clean up my mess, I decide it's time to pay the man a visit. Fortunately, my older brother is a federal judge and can get me a release waiver in a few hours.

Once I've made the right phone calls and the janitor has cleaned up, I make the drive out to the Tombs.

The Manhattan-based jail is one imposing, scary shithole: two blocky towers of concrete and steel with rows of short windows. People commit suicide there just from being kept for a few days. The idea amuses me: trash taking itself out is a goddamn public service.

Weak people are terrified of the place. It doesn't bother me—I'm not criminal, so what do I have to fear? The man I'm coming to see probably doesn't feel any fear either, thanks to being a cool-as-a-cucumber sociopath, but I'm sure he'll be eager to get away from jail.

In fact, I'm counting on it.

I sign in, present my ID and paperwork, and go to the interview room they've set up for me. There are two big, muscular, nervous-looking guards standing outside the room's door. They've already brought him; I can see the guy sitting placidly at the interview table.

"Did the warden give you the lowdown about this guy?" One of the cops, a little older and darker than the other, looks ready to stop me, but puts his hand down when I eye him.

"My agent was the one who brought him in. I'm briefed. Now let me in the damn room." I'm annoyed with these fuckers already.

Also, I need a cigarette. I quit for a while because Maggie wouldn't stop nagging me, but then she lost a tit, and I stopped caring. Her rack was part of why I married her, after all, and if she wasn't keeping up her end, why should I?

Anyway, she's gone now, so I'm back to two or three packs a day. I'm stinking up the house she was once so protective of. I'm having a nicotine blast.

Unfortunately, that's woken my cravings back up and the discomfort that hits whenever I can't light up. Which is a shitload of places in New York City. So, I'm a little on edge as he lets me into the interview room.

The older man at the table doesn't look like an infamous assassin; he looks like a retired librarian. Small, neat, graying, olive skin, and immaculately trimmed hair and nails. His eyes are warm brown, but empty.

When he sees me, he smiles and folds his hands on the tabletop as if it's natural, instead of his hands being cuffed together. "Assistant Director Daniels, how nice to see you again. To what do I owe the pleasure?"

It won't be difficult to manufacture an "escape" as soon as he's in my hands. All he needs to do is leave a few bruises on me and take my gun with him. And it won't be difficult to pass him off as traveling to Baltimore to take out Moss as a simple act of personal revenge.

"Unfinished business." My lips stretch into a big, gloating smile. "I'm here to make a deal."

He frowns slightly. "I do hope you're not expecting me to testify against anyone."

"No, it's not about that. It's about Carolyn Moss. A mutual pain in our asses." I stare at him meaningfully.

Assante's eyebrows rise, and his polite smile widens slightly as I settle into the chair across from him. "Oh? Do tell."

CHAPTER 8

Adrian

When I get back to my desk in the computer hub, the number on the wall has jumped by twenty-three people. Twenty-three successes. I'm still preoccupied with the prospect of telling Carolyn the whole truth, and the sight of that increasing number lifts my spirits, as it always does.

What bothers me the most is that I will eventually have to tell her that I am DuBois. That's not my real name, of course, but it is that of the man that she's hunting. I'm not even French.

I have become the FBI's white whale, a legend that they all whisper about but know little of the facts on. In the rumors, I have been blamed for everything from the crisis in Afghanistan to the fall of the twin towers to the current widespread investigation of pedophiles in the Catholic Church. Ironically, none of these are true. But they capture the imagination, and that makes them spread.

Fresh out of Quantico, Carolyn is intelligent and perceptive, but also inexperienced and impressionable. She will have paid attention to all the rumors as she is keenly interested in anything that can help her advance her career honorably. Even though she may not be able to look at my face in her file without blushing, she still might believe the rumors that demonize me as much as those that lionize me.

Nevertheless, all is not lost. Perhaps she will be receptive to my reasons and forgive me my deceit. She seemed to understand when I told her that DuBois was out of her reach and even to speculate on "his" lack of actionable offenses.

Perhaps she will even forgive me for being DuBois when it finally comes to light.

She already suspects than my reach is far longer than she ever imagined. She is seeing the ease with which I collect information, and she may have started to understand the reasons for my sometimes-unorthodox advice. But I have no idea how she will react when she realizes the full truth.

Perhaps the best thing I can do is to simply come clean to her when she arrives on Saturday night. I'm getting tired of withholding the information from her that she so craves.

I'm not ready to show her my face until I know she's willing to leave the FBI. I want to know the truth of her allegiances and whether her ideals are more important to her than her status as a law enforcement officer.

She may not want to leave. I cannot provide her with any status to replace it, unless of course she will allow me to take her as my wife. Of course, then her status will largely transfer to be among those that she once hunted.

How ironic.

Then I realize what thought just ran through my head, and I grumble in exasperation. Wife? Ridiculous. I'm not thinking straight right now.

My phone rings suddenly, and I recognize the ringtone for Jefferson, the man who I have installed in Derek Daniels's office as a janitor. It's a little bit late for him to be calling, unless of course there is an emergency. I pick up at once.

"Sir," he stammers in a low, terrified voice. "We have a problem."

At once, I snap to full alertness. "Go on."

"You told me to intercept any outgoing documents from his desk. He's registered some kind of legal permission form to take a prisoner out of federal custody for use in a case. I'll send over the copies I took."

"Good, thank you, but please cut to the chase. What has you phoning me up this late? Who is the prisoner?" Cold suspicion wells up in me.

He takes a moment to calm himself. "It's Assante, sir."

I close my eyes, a cold shiver running through my body as my preoccupied mind snaps to full awareness. Carolyn is in danger.

"Thank you, Mr. Jefferson. I'll wire your bonus in a few minutes. Keep monitoring and do not be concerned. Assante will not be staying in New York City." I can't keep the tension out of my voice now either.

"Thank you, sir." Relief fills every word. "I'll keep an eye out."

Once the call ends with Jefferson, I go to visit my sister. Marissa is predictably lying in her room with a towel over her eyes, recovering from the massive case of eye strain she has given herself by working ten hours straight. She's always doing this.

"Marissa, I am very sorry to disturb your rest, but we have an emergency." I stand just outside the half-open door, not entering until given leave.

She sits up at once, snatching the towel off her face. "I forgive you. What's the problem?"

I square my shoulders, pushing the door open fully. "Daniels has set loose against Carolyn an assassin with a grudge. I need you to work with the staff to make some preparations."

Most of the time, my staff is very careful to stay out of my way. I do not like being interrupted or having my conversations listened in on. Of course, all of them are trustworthy people, but even trustworthy people are only human.

Her brows draw together. "Well, I can get in touch with the security staff, but they are about the only ones on duty right now. Unless you want me to run back to the quarters and start waking people up." She doesn't sound happy with that idea, and I shake my head.

The servants' quarters are a neat little condominium complex at the back of the property. I like my privacy, and I imagine that after working all day, my staff likes it, too. Regardless of our difference in status, they are not "the help." They are human beings.

"I don't need them to handle the actual emergency, only help with some household adjustments. Talk to Marco and his seconds tonight and then we'll brief the regular staff tomorrow morning. I'm bringing Carolyn here." There's no way that I am letting Assante harm her.

"Does she know that you are bringing her here?" Marissa sounds amused, but her attempt at a tease falls flat as I stare at her. "Sorry."

"I forgive you. And no, she does not know yet. But I'm certain that she will follow my advice." She may balk at becoming my guest, but right now, her best chance of survival is to obey me.

"So, what do I tell the guards?" My sister gets up, rubbing one temple and blinking.

"I will come up with a short set of instructions and send it to you. But the primary concern is that no one in this house, including yourself, use my name around her. Anyone who does so is to be immediately sacked."

"What's the concern?" And then it seems to slowly dawn on her. "Wait … you still haven't told her that you're DuBois?"

"No, I haven't." I move forward into the doorway. "I will have to take steps to prevent her from making the connection just yet. Her loyalties are in flux right now, and as much as I want to, I am not yet certain that I can trust her that deeply."

"Brother, look. This is starting to worry me. I know she's here to hunt you under this crime lord identity of yours. But do you really think she'll go through with turning you in after everything that you have done for her?" She moves toward me, troubled.

Suddenly a little more of that cognac seems like a good idea. "That is entirely the problem, dear sister. I don't know yet. She is under tremendous pressure, and I can only hope to win her loyalty completely before she finds out."

"If you handle it that way," she warns me, "she's going to be pissed off at you for hiding the truth from her."

My mind is already rushing ahead to what I'm going to say to Carolyn, and how I'm going to entice or persuade her to come into my hands. "That is inevitable at this point, Marissa. I wish it wasn't."

She frowns. "Okay, play it your way, and I'll back you up. But remember I said that."

"Thank you for your concern. I will be down in the computer hub if you need me. Expect the list of instructions for the security staff within ten minutes." I turn on my heel and walk away, headed back downstairs.

On my walk down the hall, I weigh my options. It might be best to simply give her the truth and tell her I'm bringing her under my protection. Or I could sugar the pill.

That idea is more appealing. It will be much easier to convince her to make that leap of faith in me if she has a positive reason as well as a negative one. And I know that the both of us have feelings for each other.

Denying the influence of my emotions in this matter and considering them a distraction have been my habit since this started. But perhaps they can be a positive force. Perhaps our attraction to each other is key to drawing her into my hands.

Perhaps the only way to truly guarantee her loyalty is to win her heart. And the most expedient way to do so, besides showing her more of my true nature, is to care for the needs of her body.

Poor, hard-working Carolyn. She has no idea that I'm the one who substituted four out of the five men on Daniels's list without his ever even knowing it. I chose those men not only because they were on the verge of renouncing their destructive tendencies and would lead her to bigger fish, but because of their beauty.

That was a bit cruel of me, to entice and fluster her like that. But I wanted to get an idea of what kind of man interested her and also to try to get through to her that not a one of them truly deserved to spend their lives in prison. Beauty and goodness are inextricably linked in the human subconscious.

When I sit back down at my desk, the number hung on the wall has increased by another seven people. I will have to show this to Carolyn in the course of my explaining myself. Nothing encapsulates my purposes or my ideals more.

But for now, arrangements must be made to allow her to live in my home safely, and perhaps even share my bed, without ever laying eyes on me.

That is going to be interesting all by itself.

CHAPTER 9

Carolyn

*M*y phone rings a few minutes after midnight, and I pick it up at once. "Pack your things and prepare to move out of your hotel room," Prometheus states quickly, not even pausing for a greeting. "It's no longer safe for you there."

"What's going on?" I sit up in my bed, clutching the blankets to my chest out of old habit.

"Carolyn, there is no time for an explanation. Please follow my instructions. There will be a car waiting for you downstairs in five minutes." His voice is so terribly grave that it grabs my full attention.

Something is really wrong.

"I'll be there." There is no way of knowing what it's going to look like to the other FBI agents when I vanish in the middle of the night. But on the other hand, they should never have been involved in my problems in the first place.

"Good. We will be speaking in person soon enough." He hangs up, and I set my phone down slowly, heart suddenly in my throat.

Oh my God, he wants to meet. Not only that, but he's trying to protect me from something. Daniels? DuBois?

Hastily packing up, I wish he had at least hinted at the reason behind his urgency. Obviously there has to be some kind of a serious crisis going on for him to change his mind about meeting me so fast.

Passing the bathroom mirror, I wince. I'm in a plain pair of jogging pants and T-shirt right now—not the impression I want to make on the man who curls my toes with just his voice. But apparently, there's no time to fix it.

There is a full-blown thunderstorm going on again when I walk out the front door of the hotel. Sheets of water fall from the front and sides of the awning, obscuring the street. A few blocks off, a blackout has plunged a neighborhood into darkness, suddenly ending the string of streetlights.

Not even a minute later, a limousine arrives. Its black form noses in under the awning and comes to a stop directly in front of me. The door opens and a woman in her early twenties leans out, her black bob swinging on either side of her narrow face.

"Hi!" she says cheerfully. "I'm Marissa. Get in. We need to get out of here before the storm gets any worse."

That confuses me. Is there a natural disaster coming? Is the hotel built in a floodplain?

There's no time to ask questions just yet. I grab my suitcase and hurry over to the car, slipping inside. I make sure to shut the door and buckle up before asking, "What's going on?"

"Prometheus found out that there's someone after you, and they're arriving in town in about half an hour. It's really important you be long gone out of this hotel before then." She leans forward and grabs a

71

bottle of iced tea out of the limousine's mini-fridge. "You want something to drink?"

"Just information. My stomach's bad." The sudden awakening and subsequent unnerving news has me queasy. "What's your relationship with Prometheus?"

She laughs. "He's my older brother. Sorry about all the weirdness. He is being very hush-hush about things right now, because he's not quite sure if he can trust you fully yet. Don't be offended. He's that paranoid toward everyone he doesn't know well."

"I noticed." I'm not offended, just glad that even if it's an emergency prompting it, Prometheus is finally letting me in a little. "So, who did he find out is after me?"

"Assante."

No. The news hits like a bucket of icy water. "But he's in jail! He's locked up in the Tombs. I put his ass there myself—"

She smiles apologetically. "Yeah, probably why he wants to kill you now. Prometheus told me to tell you that Daniels used his older brother, a federal judge, to get the paperwork signed to get Assante out so that he could use him in an investigation."

I rub my throbbing temple, stunned. "I am familiar with the protocol. And your brother is probably right. Logically, if Daniels got him out, he's sending Assante after me."

"Well, don't worry. If there is one thing that my brother is good at besides computers, it's privacy and security. We're going to stash you someplace where Assante can't possibly find you." She has a slightly too mischievous face for her smile to be reassuring, but she seems to mean well.

"I still can't believe this." It's hard to draw a full breath. "If Daniels is going this far, he must not care anymore about the consequences. He can't possibly think having me murdered isn't going to go unnoticed, can he? It'll be traced back to him with ease."

"Well, that's the thing about stupid people. They always think that they're smarter than everyone else." She leans back in her seat, her gaze flicking over me. "Anyway, apparently Daniels played it so that it looked like Assante escaped from his custody."

"Oh. How did he make that believable?" My hands are numb from shock; rubbing them together just makes them prickle uncomfortably.

"Well, either he had Assante beat him up, or he went out and got himself mugged." She takes a swallow of her drink. "We have a witness who says he came back to your office via the hospital, all bandaged up."

"That covers his butt for now." Now that the shock is starting to wear off, the bitterness is setting in. "Where are we going?"

"Our place!" She gives an impish grin at my surprised look. "My brother wants to meet with you, and after that we have a room prepared so you can get some sleep."

"Wow. I'm sorry. It's just very surprising. Back in Detroit, he refused to meet with me." Apparently, it was pointless to take that personally, as sad as his rejection made me then. He's just ... like that.

"Well, my brother takes a long time to warm up to people. He takes even longer to trust anyone. He didn't even fully trust me when he met me, and we have the same father." She gestures toward me with the bottle. "He really likes you. And he wants you to be safe."

That warm feeling starts to trickle into me again even through my fear over the whole Assante situation. Last time with Assante, it was two on one. Another highly trained professional assassin softened him up for me before I even got on scene. Facing him alone would probably end in my death.

But now, I'm not alone. Prometheus isn't just meeting with me, and he's not just helping me. He's taking me into his home to protect me.

Nobody's ever done anything like that for me before. "I appreciate it, but it confuses me. Prometheus said he finds me interesting, and an FBI agent is a good ally to have when you're a hacker. But—"

Her sudden laugh startles me. "Oh wow, you really have no idea."

"No idea about what?"

Her eyes are dancing as she smiles at me, like she's keeping the best secret in the world and can barely contain it. "My brother is in love with you, honey. He's barely willing to admit it to himself, let alone to me. But until you came along, we were pretty much each other's only loved ones. He's never been like this over a woman before."

I just sit there blinking at her. What do you even say to that?

I thought he just wanted to have sex with me. But I can't exactly say that to his sister. "He hasn't even met me."

She takes another big swallow of her tea. "My brother connects with people online all the time, Agent Moss. To him, a really positive online relationship is more valuable than a less positive relationship in person."

"I don't even know his name." Outside, the storm is getting stronger, obscuring everything beyond the windowpane with a thick layer of rain. The glass is cool as I lean the side of my forehead against it.

Is this a dream? No, my damn head hurts too much for it to possibly be a dream. This is real, and Prometheus isn't just interested or fascinated or wanting to fuck me. Little sister is smiling as she spills the tea on him.

He has fallen for me, too, long distance, without ever having met in person. And now we're about to meet. And somehow, that makes Daniels sending a very angry and very dangerous assassin after me a little less scary.

"He's worried about how you're going to react to certain things about him, like his name and appearance. His appearance especially. It's kinda distinctive." There's a note of apology in her words.

74

"Is he disfigured? Is that why he's so reclusive?" That doesn't matter to me when there's so much about him to want.

"No. Look, he'll explain everything to you. Just please, be a little patient. He's really eccentric, but he also really cares about you." Despite her merry smile, her eyes plead with me.

"If what you're saying is true, then he's trying to save my life. Patience is not a problem. But I really don't know how to take all of this. How does he plan to meet with me if he doesn't want me to see his face?"

The sudden mental image of Prometheus showing up in a mask like he's from The Phantom of the Opera pops into my head. A little ridiculous, but not implausible. It wouldn't be any more eccentric than some of the other things he's done.

"You guys will figure something out when you get there." She hesitates and then becomes much more serious. "There's just one thing."

"What's that?" We're heading away from the city center. How far is their home from Baltimore?

"You need to understand that my brother pulled me out of a hellish situation when I was little, and without him, I wouldn't have anything. If something starts up between you and him, that's all good with me, but ..."

Her eyes are steady on mine, and her voice is getting more and more grave. It reminds me so much of Prometheus's when he told me to start packing that it catches my strict attention.

"But ...?" My question comes out as gently as possible.

"But if you hurt him, if you betray his trust or rat him out or screw up his life, I'm going to forget that I'm starting to like you already, and I will go all out to ruin you." Her eyes flash as she meets my glance; it's clear she means everything she says. And who could blame her?

My voice comes out thick with emotion. "I don't want to hurt him. That's about the last thing on my mind. You have to understand. He's not just someone I owe a lot to or who I'm attracted to. He's the one man I've been able to rely on. No way will I turn around and answer what he's done for me with betrayal. It's understandable that he doesn't quite trust me yet, and that you don't quite trust me yet. The trust issues are pretty mutual, actually. But I want there to be trust. I'm ... so tired of not having anyone."

It's a relief to finally get these feelings off my chest, and it also helps me sort them out. It's kind of weird to be having this intimate of a conversation with a near stranger, but this woman appears completely earnest in her protectiveness toward her brother. She could be a brilliant actress, but micro-expressions don't lie, and neither does body language.

I'm still an investigator, relying on training and instincts. Right now, my instincts are saying that this is an honest conversation that needs to happen in order for me to truly understand the situation.

And yet, it's risky with so many unknowns. Is this all some sort of elaborate game Prometheus has been playing with me? Is this woman here to help him manipulate me?

Is he using her honest, protective, sisterly love for him to help him manipulate me?

I want to trust the wonderful, warm, unfamiliar feeling that blooms inside of me whenever Prometheus shows that he cares about me. It's so seductive, tempting something deep inside my heart that has never been satisfied.

It also turns me right the hell on. Which again is an unfamiliar feeling.

If this man can make my body respond just with his beautiful voice, what will he be able to do once we're alone together?

She breaks his silence by leaning forward. "Well, I hope that's true, because believe me, it's too late to talk any sense into my brother. Of course, he'd be furious if he knew that I'm sticking my nose in like this, but it really is for his own good. And yours, apparently.

"It may take him a while to actually admit how he feels, just to warn you. But you wanted to know why he's doing all of this, and that's why. I'm sure he also thinks you're hot—holy shit, you are blushing hard, honey." She covers her mouth with her hand.

I can't look at her for a moment.

"I know this is awkward, but I swear, it's for a good cause. And I'll probably be telling him the same thing when he finds out that I told you all this."

"It's ... okay. If I had a brother who really cared about me, I would probably do the same thing. Well, I might be a little bit more subtle about it."

She starts snickering, coaxing out my smile.

"That's good." She drains the rest of her bottle of tea and pulls a recyclables drawer out from under the seat beside her, tossing it in. "One last thing, though."

"What's that?" I start digging in my shoulder bag for my bottle of aspirin.

"That thing you said about your value to him as an FBI agent? Honey, Prometheus doesn't need another FBI agent in his corner. He's got dozens. And not because he's corrupted them. You'll see. My brother just wants you for you. Not for what you can give him. That's the bottom line."

She goes quiet for a few minutes, giving me a chance to process all this. She passes me a bottle of water to wash down my aspirin, and I drink it slowly, watching the storm as we drive.

"So, tell me about this Assante guy," she finally says as we reach the outskirts of Baltimore.

I pull my gaze away from the dark, storm-tossed countryside, frowning. "Assante is the man who the Cohen mob family in Las Vegas sends when one of their regular hitmen has to be taken out. Before that, he was a free agent with a very high kill count. He's been in the business for decades.

"When assassins last long enough to get old, you know they're really dangerous. Assante is in his sixties. He's Sicilian-born, and even with our spotty information, we have linked him to dozens of murders."

"Wow. That's pretty intense. Go on." Marissa's eyes are fixed intently on my face, not blinking much, which is a little unnerving. She reminds me of a cat.

"When I crossed paths with Assante, I was in Mexico, having followed my latest assignment there. The suspect's name was Brian Stone, and he was a much less well-known Cohen hitter who was trying to escape the life. I was well out of my jurisdiction anyway, so I was perfectly willing to let Stone go.

"But as for Assante, he very nearly murdered an innocent woman and a small child right in front of me. So, I let Brian Stone beat the crap out of him, helped subdue him, and then bound him up in duct tape, stuck him in the trunk of my rental car—"

"Whoa, wait. Hold the phone. You did what? Holy shit!" Her shoulders are shaking, and there are tears with the corners of her eyes. "No wonder this guy wants to kill you!"

"Yeah, I kind of let myself get too pissed off at him when he threatened that kid. He really did deserve it though." And even though now it has him on a single-minded path of revenge against me, it's still funny.

"Well, nobody's happy that this guy is in town looking for you, of course. But this isn't exactly our first time dealing with hitters. The last Don of New York City hated my brother. He had to monitor the damn airport all the time for a few years, just because they were coming down the coast that often gunning for us."

That's a weird coincidence. "You mean, the Don who was just assassinated at the Canadian border?"

"Yeah." She nods and looks out the window as lightning flashes. "That's the one. We were both really glad when that guy kicked the bucket."

Something clicks in my head, and I start to wonder. The first man on the list of suspects that Daniels gave me was a car thief who randomly rescued that Don's runaway daughter from a retrieval team. But was it really random?

The Don was so furious that when his daughter was located by his men in Montreal, he came up there himself despite being terrified of the local crime lord. Not only did he fail to retrieve his daughter, but he was forced to flee back toward the States out of fear that the Sixth Family was about to crush him for trespassing in their territory.

But before he could cross back safely into his own territory, an assassin killed him at the border, very likely on the orders of the Don of Montreal. That assassin coincidentally turned out to be the second man on my list. The second man on my list then attempted to flee the Sixth Family, only to end up hunted by them in Massachusetts.

The second man was a near complete amnesiac, thanks to one of the murder attempts against him. He was no help in providing information about his former employers, but he was perfectly willing to lead the men hunting him into a trap. I then made the collar, and the men were eventually extradited back to Canada.

The third man on my list was the one who had tried to escape the Cohens. I don't yet know if there's any connection between him and the others. But he is the one whose escape attempt brought Assante into my life—a Sicilian-expatriate assassin, like the second man on my list.

Is that a coincidence or another connection between the cases?

The capture of Assante was my most high-profile collar to date and a brilliant way to jumpstart my career at the bureau. Or at least it would have been, if Daniels wasn't constantly sabotaging my attempts to gain any recognition.

Of course, though nobody seems to have believed him, Assante was very quick to point out that the way I got him back across the border was as illegal as it was undignified. That is true. Going on this twisting path has left me ethically compromised in some ways by bureau standards.

But comparing myself to someone like Daniels, who still holds an administrative position while he's being investigated for mass sexual harassment ... I am as pure as the driven snow.

The fourth man on my list was in Detroit. What a disaster that was. He was an underground mixed martial arts fighter suspected of killing two men in the ring.

As it turned out, one of those men had died from a drug overdose, and the other death was purely an accident. And yet, while I was investigating this relatively innocent man, a violent serial stalker, who had just attempted to murder a young woman and was rescued by the fighter, ended up in my sights instead. He was also a hacker who set himself up as a rival to Prometheus.

Prometheus apparently did some work for the owner of the underground fighting league. I spent an extra month in Detroit looking for him after his name was mentioned, but he wouldn't permit a meeting. My guess is that like me, he has been wrestling with his feelings.

But his sister doesn't entirely have the right impression of him either. She doesn't believe that her brother could be using me because he cares for me so much. I wish that were true but looking back over the last four cases shows me how often there are connections to Prometheus.

And here we are in Baltimore, where Prometheus lives. And the last one on my list is also here: DuBois. My best guess is, he's Prometheus' rival, ally, or possibly an employer.

All roads lead back to this man who supposedly loves me. No wonder he knew so much about the suspects—he's involved with each of them somehow.

It's not clear how Prometheus could have engineered some of the things that have happened during these cases. But if I'm right, he has benefited directly from almost everything he has done to help me with them.

The Don who tried to kill him and his sister on a regular basis is now dead in part because of me. The hacker who tried to expose a business that he was associated with was imprisoned in part because of me. Prometheus has taken advantage of my attempts to complete my assignments to achieve some of his own goals.

It's difficult for me to be angry about it, since I would never have minded helping him in return for his assistance. But it bothers me that he has been apparently playing this game and concealed at least some of his true motives. It makes it more difficult for me to trust him.

But I still want to see him. Desperately.

"You must be pretty tired," she notices, and I nod distractedly. "Don't worry. We're almost there."

"Where is 'there'?" We are far out enough in the countryside now that the actual lights from buildings are starting to get few and far between. The driver slows the limousine and turns us onto a pristine private road that runs back into the low hills.

"Out past the nature preserve. My brother's got a lot of land out here."

"May I ask you a question?" I turn to watch her face.

She nods. "Shoot."

"Why did Prometheus send you out here instead of just having the driver pick me up?" It's fortunate that he did, but also a little risky for her if Assante is on his way.

"I totally volunteered for it." She gives that mischievous smile again. "I wanted to learn more about you, and Prometheus really wanted to make sure that you were in good hands. Who better than his own sister?"

That brings a small smirk to my face. "That and you wanted to give me a little 'I'll kick your ass if you hurt my brother' speech."

That gets me another laugh. "Oh yeah, definitely. We should be there in a minute, by the way. It's about a quarter-mile up the road."

The storm is even worse out here, making it hard for me to see much on the road ahead. Finally, however, I glimpse lights through a break in the low trees.

I already started to suspect that Prometheus is independently wealthy when he started sending me gifts. When I saw the limousine, I was certain of it. But now, as the sprawling estate house swings into view ahead, what pops into my mind is, this guy doesn't have to work for anyone else.

He is very obviously already a billionaire. And the sight of his palatial home just reminds me there is so much about him that is a total mystery to me.

CHAPTER 10

Carolyn

The place is quiet when we get in. Almost nobody seems to be around. The driver helps with my luggage, and a man with a cart is waiting for my suitcase when we walk inside the foyer, but that's it.

Oddly, the tall, spiky-haired man helping me with my luggage has a gun on his belt. Is he part of security staff? Maybe they're the only ones up.

I can understand. I'm exhausted. All the excitement and the long car ride, along with that unexpected soul-searching conversation with Marissa, has left me drained. So, has finally connecting some of the dots about Prometheus, his interest in me, and the last four cases.

The place is big enough that it has its own elevator. Marissa rides it with me and the security guard, chattering about the building and its history the whole time. It's tough to focus on what she's saying.

It's a lovely old house, but it's far less important to me than the man living here—the man I have never met, but who somehow has become more important to me in three short months than almost anyone.

The room that they have set aside for me is the same size as my entire apartment back in New York City. It has its own en suite bathroom, a huge canopy bed, a desk with an ethernet cable waiting, and balcony windows overlooking a dark, sprawling garden. On the bed is a manila envelope.

"Okay, so, gonna leave you guys to talk. He will be in to see you in about twenty minutes. I'll see you at breakfast." Marissa gives me a last smile and walks out, her boot heels clicking down the hall.

I grab my suitcase and pull it open, looking for a clean change of clothes that is actually more presentable than my sleeping outfit. I finally pull out a velvet skirt set with a long tunic top, both in midnight blue. No point bothering with shoes or jewelry.

The en suite bathroom is on the small side but beautiful, done up in gold fixtures, with tiles the color of piano keys. I shower off and wash my hair with jasmine-scented soap.

Coming out of the bathroom, showered and changed, I half expect there to be a man in a mask sitting on the bed. Instead, the only thing there is that mysterious manila envelope. I sit down on the bed and open it up.

Out falls a wide black silk blindfold, so sleek and fine that it slips out of my fingers when I try to catch it. A small, folded bit of note paper flutters to the forest-green comforter after it. The handwriting is beautiful and familiar looking.

Put this on.

I hesitate and then pick up the blindfold and tie it over my eyes. It's wide enough that I can see no light above or below it. I sit there, fighting my nervousness, waiting for something to happen.

Almost instantly, the door opens. The heavy, purposeful tread of a large man enters the room, and I catch a whiff of his sandalwood cologne. He approaches me and then pulls a chair over across the floor. It creaks heavily as he settles into it; he must be huge.

"Good evening, Carolyn." Prometheus's deep, soft, musical voice has even more power up close. It instantly leaves me weak in the knees.

"Hello." My voice comes out tiny and breathless.

"I'm going to set down some ground rules for our interactions. Please do not deviate from them if you wish these interactions to continue." I hear a rustle of his clothing. It sounds like silk.

"I understand." Why is this so exciting?

"Do you know the legend of Cupid and Psyche, Carolyn?"

I have to think hard for a moment. His voice has me under its spell. "Yes. He required her to meet him in total darkness and never try to look at him, or he would leave."

"Good. My requirements are similar. For your safety as well as mine, do not remove the blindfold while we are together. I will decide when to reveal myself to you. Do not attempt to push the issue. You're not to give the location of this place to anyone. You're not to bring guests back here. If you find it necessary to leave the compound, you will make sure that you're not followed back." A pause. "That is all."

"I understand." Most of his conditions are to be expected, if he's trying to hide his identity.

anywhere in the house but the basement, which is where
and the two upper floors, which are my living
be changed as you show yourself trust-
mix of gentle and stern, neither

still dead curious about whatever he's
his privacy, and his rules. And I don't

85

mind him laying down the law with me. In fact, the whole idea intrigues me.

"What else do you want from me?" My voice is still embarrassingly girlish and breathy, giving away too much.

"What would you offer me?" he asks softly, his tone a touch more ... intense.

Me. I start to tremble but can't say the words aloud. You can have me.

I hear him get up from the chair, looming over me. His scent, his gentle breathing, the warmth running through me, all make me swoon so hard that I can barely prop myself upright on my hands.

His effect on me, my loneliness, that emotional conversation with Marissa, and the fact that my life is in peril all mix inside of me until I am dizzy from it all. Finally, I give up and gasp, "I just want you to touch me."

A long-fingered hand suddenly brushes against the side of my face, cupping my cheek. Those smooth, tapered fingers slide back against my hair, which is still held tight in its braid. He cups the nape of my neck very gently; my head tilts back into his hand, and my lips part to let in a shivery breath.

Warm breath slides over my face and then something smooth and warm brushes against my lips, leaving behind a tingle. My pussy clenches suddenly, hard, my whole body lighting up with pleasure and desire. I lean blindly after the kiss—and his mouth comes down on mine hungrily.

I throw my arms around his neck and pull him closer, suddenly greedy, standing up from the bed to press my body against one that is huge and warm and firmly muscled. His hands slide up and down my back, his tongue slides delicately against mine, and when I have stop and catch my breath, he starts kissing my neck instead.

His lips, gentle on my skin, send electric jolts of unfamiliar through me. My startled moan draws a chuckle from

"Don't stop," I whisper, and he pulls me closer and starts using his tongue to trace the cords in my neck. "Do you want me to make love to you?" he murmurs against my pulse.

I go still for a moment, one encouraging hand around his back and the other in his hair. "I've never …" I whisper. "But … yes …"

"Oh," he breathes, almost reverently. "Then I should make it something to remember."

He kisses me deeply again, his slim fingers wandering down to caress my breast through the fabric. When they brush over my nipple, it tightens almost painfully, and I whimper.

"You may touch me anywhere but my face," he instructs, his voice gone deeper and shaking just a little. He moves away, hands sliding off me again. "I'm going to take my clothes off now. I'm finding them suddenly … confining."

I hear fabric rustle, and the warm scent of his skin gets a little stronger. His breathing roughens as I eagerly reach forward to find him pulling off a shirt and sweater. My fingertips find his tight, rippled belly as he stretches, and they slide over it eagerly.

"Unbuckle my belt," he pants softly. The leather is stiff, but I tug it free and unfasten it obediently. My fingers wander lower, and he sucks air as they encounter a hard, throbbing bulge under the cloth.

"Unzip me," he purrs needlessly; I eagerly tug his zipper down and reach inside to feel the silky cloth of a pair of boxer briefs. The outline of his cock pushes the fabric out; I run my fingertips down its length, and he lets out a little moan.

"You first, my darling." His pants hit the floor, and a moment later, he moves up to me and starts unbuttoning my tunic.

I fumble to help, eagerly shrugging out of it, shivering just a touch as the cool air hits me. I have dreamed of this too long to back away now.

87

He buries his face in my cleavage, kissing my breastbone and darting his hot tongue down between my breasts. I pull him close eagerly, stretching against him, my nipples burning with the unfamiliar need to feel his mouth. "More," I whimper.

He lifts his head, breathing, "Take your bra off."

I eagerly reach back to remove it and offer him my breasts. He covers them with kisses, holding me up as my legs get wobbly. He tastes me all over, his tongue swirling and lashing closer and closer to my nipples as I dig my nails against his shoulders and sob.

I never believed anything could feel this good. He's stoking an unfamiliar fire in me, one that grows hotter and hotter every time his tongue lashes against my nipple. I pump my hips with each movement of his mouth—and finally he cups my pussy one-handed so that he presses against it firmly every time I squirm.

Finally, he starts sucking hard, lifting me completely off my feet in his eagerness, his arms wrapped firmly around my hips. When we fall back onto the bed together, I grab the blindfold with one hand to keep it from dislodging.

He's made it clear. If I lay eyes on his face before he's ready to show it to me, we're done. And right now, I would do anything to keep this going.

I've never had a near-naked man pressed against me before. His skin is smooth and warm, his body flexes and shivers under my fingertips, and his cock digs gently against my thigh. There is tremendous power in the body shuddering against mine, but his touch never gets too rough.

"Carolyn." His hoarse whisper sounds almost reverent. As I stroke his hair, it hits me: Marissa was right. He's stuck on me, though we've barely just met in person.

My heart lightens and fills with tenderness. "Help me out of these clothes."

Somehow, it's easier with the blindfold. As he slides my panties off my hips, I can't see my own naked skin, and that makes me feel less exposed.

"I'm leaving the stockings," he informs me, his hands stroking my thighs just above their tops.

I shiver and nod mutely as he settles between my legs. I feel bare flesh; he's abandoned the last of his clothes. The smooth head of his cock brushes against my mound. I brace myself for a sudden entry.

Instead, he takes his throbbing organ in hand and runs the head up and down my slit, then opens me delicately and starts stroking my inner lips the same way. The sensation makes me rock my hips gently against him, and he stiffens slightly with pleasure.

"We're going to play a little game," he murmurs in my ear as he looms over me, still teasing me with the head of his cock. "I won't go any deeper than you tell me to."

He braces himself above me, and gently tucks the head of his cock, now slick with my juices, into the entrance of my aching cunt. "Mmm. Now. Let's get you a little more excited ..."

Two of his fingers slide in between my pussy lips, just above his thick head, and start slowly, very delicately stroking me. My eyes fly open behind the blindfold and I arch against him, "Oh!"

I have never felt a sensation like this before. It rockets through me, almost painfully intense, making my muscles tighten. It scares me, but I crave more.

"There we are." His musical voice has grown deep and whispery with lust. "Would you like me to go deeper inside of you?"

I roll my hips upward invitingly. "Yes ..."

He sinks into me a little further, letting out a contented sigh. "Delicious. Now, a little farther ..."

His fingertips slip up a little farther, and the sensation rocks through me again. It would scare me if I didn't want it so badly; I press up against his fingers. "More …"

He strokes me faster, fingertips swirling now, so slick from my juices that they move without pain over my most sensitive spot. His cock sinks deeper in, and our soft moans mix in the air.

I wrap my legs around his hips, clinging to him as his fingers steadily caress me. My inner muscles tighten around his shaft as he pushes against me, filling me almost completely now. His hips hitch against me slightly as he fights the urge to thrust.

His fingertips work against my aching clit until every single swirl around it feels better than the last. My nails are in his back now; my body has locked up, and my thoughts are focusing in on the mounting sensations.

"Just like that … yes …" My muscles tighten further, and I groan through my teeth. "Fuck me …"

He starts moving his hips finally, gasping as he draws out of me and plunges in again. He moves slowly but powerfully, his whole body flexing and tensing with pleasure on each thrust. His fingers keep stroking me, driving me into a frenzy. My breath comes out in hoarse cries that get louder as I rise toward ecstasy.

Then, he pushes me that extra fraction, and all that tension releases deliciously in long waves. He thrusts deep, groaning as my muscles caress him, until my body settles down, leaving me blissed out and half conscious. He pushes hard against me, and his cock jumps and shudders inside of me.

He holds himself rigid, panting though his teeth as he trembles with ecstasy. Then he sags over me with a soft sigh and leans down to nuzzle my cheek.

"You are worth any risk," he tells me as I lie there limp, overwhelmed by sudden, soft exhaustion.

I drift off before he can even draw his cock out of me.

I wake up still wearing the blindfold and nothing else. I'm warm and snuggly under fine, smooth covers, and Prometheus is lying beside me with one arm thrown over me. His soft breathing tells me that he's asleep.

I lift my head, then settle back down, reluctant to move much. I'm refreshed, but so relaxed and so reluctant to leave his arms.

That's when it hits me. He's asleep.

I could very easily solve the mystery of why he doesn't want me looking at his face right now.

I could just tug it aside and take a quick peek. He'll never know.

But then I remember his warnings and how he is trusting me. I sigh ... and lay my head on his chest instead, wrapping my arm around him. We'll do it your way, big guy.

CHAPTER 11

Adrian

*S*he passed the test.

I wake slowly with Carolyn curled up in my arms. Her blindfold is still on, and she is still with me.

An enormous sigh of relief escapes me, and I cuddle her closer, burying my nose in her silvery hair. I didn't expect it to be this important to me that she pass this final test, but it is. Now, I know that I can trust her enough to give her the full truth.

The only problem is, first I have to brace myself to pull away from her softness and her warmth, get dressed in the dark, and slip out of the room before she wakes up. I don't want to do any of that. I want to stay here and make love to her again.

But it's been several hours, and though I have exhausted her, her eyes will be opening soon. She will then want to use them; it's ridiculous to expect her to keep the blindfold in place all morning.

My life has been one long series of calculated risks. Starting my life-long internet project and the consolidation of my power within the American underworld was certainly a calculated risk. So was bringing Marissa into my home.

It's time to risk revealing myself to Carolyn. It's time for me to really show her my true work and the benefits of joining me. However, I know better than to subject her to the shock of waking up to the face of the man she is supposed to be hunting.

Today, however, is definitely the day. I have no more excuses. Hopefully, I have made love to her thoroughly and satisfyingly enough that she is no longer carrying so much of the stress from last night's trials.

She certainly responded that way. And she's still sleeping deeply as I slip away from her and wrap her in the blankets to help her keep warm. I press a kiss to her forehead and then reach for the spot on the floor where I dropped my clothes.

Once I dress, leave, and reach my sanctum upstairs, I shower off, enjoying how the nail marks all across my upper back sting under the pressure of the water. Her cries of pleasure from last night echo in my memory, making me smile. It's a very good start to things, even if the circumstances are ... unusual.

Except, of course, for the sense of vulnerability that haunts me as I clean up, put on a fresh dark-linen suit, and prepare to join my sister for morning coffee. It's a ritual that we have followed for the last year and a half, as our sleep schedules are very similar. Neither one of us has much of an appetite in the morning before our time in the gymnasium, and neither one of us is ever quite awake enough to work out safely without a shot of caffeine.

The small parlor on the uppermost level of the mansion is the same room where my enemy hung himself. He left himself for his poor servants to find. I kept many of them on, as they had no loyalty to him left after that, and there was no reason for their employer's misfortune to lead to theirs.

I have kept everything the same in the room except for changing the light fixture that he broke with his weight. He would probably be devastated to discover that that room is now one of my favorites in the house. The coffee service is already laid out on the room's small mahogany table as I walk in.

There is no sign that anyone died here. My enemy has disappeared without a trace. That would probably infuriate him.

Like my feelings for Carolyn, my vindictive streak has influenced many of my decisions. I don't think she needs to know that my old enemy killed himself here or that I'm the one who drove him to suicide.

She makes me wish I was a kinder person or rather that my kindness did not have to be enforced with violence at times. But that is simply not possible. The world is what it is, and a man like my former enemy is outside the reach of the law.

But he was not outside of my reach.

I sit down and wait for my sister, who is running a little late. Not a surprise after she wore herself out yesterday on her robotics project. When she comes in slowly a few minutes later, I open my mouth to tease her—only to close it when I see her face.

Pale as a ghost, she walks over to her seat, sits down, and is silent for a few seconds as she stares at me. Then she speaks breathlessly. "Well, it looks like we got your girlfriend out of that hotel just in time."

Adrenaline is so much faster-working than caffeine. I'm fully awake in less than a second. "What has happened, Marissa?"

Her lips tremble. "It just hit the news. Those four FBI agents who Daniels sent to do surveillance on Carolyn—they're dead, along with two of the hotel staff."

My blood starts to boil at once. "Assante."

"It has to be. Apparently, it happened on the fourth floor. From the security video we retrieved, he first went to the two hotel suites that were bugged." She looks sick.

I sit back in my chair heavily. "That means that either Daniels neglected to tell him Carolyn had moved suites again, or he wanted the agents dead, too."

"Why the hell would he want to cause a giant mess that would make the news, cause a big investigation, and increase the chances of it all being traced back to him?" Marissa sounds angry, probably out of worry for Carolyn. She seems to like my new love and to understand that what troubles Carolyn troubles me.

My hands are curling with the urge to strangle two very troublesome men. "Both Daniels and Assante seem to think that killing Carolyn is important enough to take the risk. And now, six undeserving people are dead."

"Yeah." She busies herself by pouring us each a cup of coffee, dropping three lumps of sugar into mine to melt and diluting hers with cream. "At least the agents put up a fight. Maybe they hurt him."

"I should have set some kind of trap for the bastard." But there was no time.

"You can't blame yourself for this." She slides me over my cup of coffee, and I take up the little silver spoon to stir the sugar into it as it melts. "Do you think there's any chance this crazy stunt is finally going to end Daniels?"

"Not quickly enough. The wheels of the federal justice system turn ridiculously slowly. If they didn't, I would be out of a job." I take a scalding swallow of coffee, and the pain helps sharpen my wits.

I have to think past all this anger. I will not be the one to make a mistake in this situation. Assante, unlike the man who sent him, is no fool. He is also going to be very hard to find after this.

I have to be at the top of my game to handle this situation. Not to mention, to handle Carolyn's grief and rage when she finds out that her four colleagues have been murdered in her stead.

"How are we going to catch the guy?" Marissa is toying with her coffee instead of drinking it, stirring it endlessly with the tiny spoon.

"That is being worked on." It hurts my pride to admit that I don't have a full plan formulated. "But first I'm going to direct every local asset and every possible bit of spare computing power toward finding Assante. He's not going to leave the area until he has successfully killed Carolyn. That means that if he thinks she's going to be somewhere, he'll go to that place." An idea starts to form in my head, but I don't like it.

It involves using Carolyn as bait.

"Carolyn's boss already knows she's going to visit the Mermaid Club this Saturday night looking for DuBois. He's sure to have told Assante." I take another swallow of the heavily sweetened coffee.

"So, what, lay a trap for him at the club? It's a public place. This guy's already shown a willingness to shoot things up and cause a crap ton of collateral damage." She looks very worried, and I don't blame her. If that tape she just watched scared her this badly, it probably brims over with carnage.

"Carnage is not Assante's usual modus operandi. He didn't live this long by being this unsubtle. Like Daniels, he's allowing his emotions to rule him, and this is causing him to make mistakes."

She puffs out her cheeks. "So how do we keep from doing the same? We're all kinds of pissed off over this." She swallows down her first cup in several long gulps and then reaches for the coffee urn again.

"We talk it over with Carolyn, we make our plans, and we make absolutely certain that the entire club is full of my people on Saturday night. Then we lure him there, and we get rid of him when he shows up." My coffee is of the highest quality, but I can't even taste it right now.

"Are you absolutely sure Carolyn is willing to take the risk of cooperating?" Her hand is a little shaky; she almost spills the coffee.

I smile grimly over the rim of my coffee mug. "She will likely be even more eager to avenge the deaths of those men than we are."

"You're probably right, big brother. But first we have to break the news to her."

My heart sinks a little. "That is true, and I'm not looking forward to it either."

It seems that revealing myself to Carolyn has to be put on hold. After everything she's been through, it's not fair to make her deal with more than one large shock at a time. And breaking the news really is going to be difficult on its own.

I absolutely cannot stand to see her cry. It's one of the reasons that I've finally been forced to admit, after over a month of walking around the issue, that I really am in love with her.

How bizarre.

And yet, it's more welcome than I could have ever imagined. Even as this crisis looms over us, there is no denying the truth. She has my heart, and in this matter, I'm the one who must dance to her tune.

At least to a degree. And it troubles me surprisingly little.

"Don't go back to sherry," Marissa pleads quietly. "None of us is going to be thinking completely straight about this already. Booze won't help."

Her worry makes me smile. "I don't need to. I have something far better for me than alcohol waiting downstairs."

She smiles a little back. "Yeah. You do. Now, you really should probably talk to her. Once you've figured out how you want to play this, let me know."

I go back down the hall to my cavernous bedroom, which is dominated by the dark, massive beams and purple velvet drapery of a medieval-style bed designed after a Frankish king's. I first saw drawings of the original when I was ten years old and promised myself that one day I would have a bed like that. Yet now, sitting down on it, I can't even enjoy sinking into its vast mattress.

I pick up my phone slowly, bracing myself. I text Carolyn first.

Are you awake?

She doesn't answer for a few moments, forcing me to do some deep breathing to fight the urge to go down there and knock on the door. Then, I get a text back.

I just looked at my news feed. They're dead.

Horrified, I call her at once. "Carolyn, I'm so sorry. I never intended for this to happen."

"This isn't your doing. It's Daniels's and Assante's." Her voice shakes with anger and grief, but it's strong and clear. "You got me out of there before he could kill me, too. You were right about Daniels going completely off the rails. We have both provoked him. But he deserved it, and in a lot of cases, it was necessary." She sniffles and rummages for something.

"There is a box of tissues in your nightstand drawer."

"Thank you." She goes quiet for a few moments. "I wish you would come down."

Not a good idea. "Carolyn, if I come down and you look me in the face, everything is going to change even more than it is right now. That will be inevitable. I will come down, if you really want me to. But it would be better to deal with this crisis first." I'm not commanding her this time. The choice is hers.

She hesitates. "Maybe you're right."

"I will show you more of me, however. Go downstairs to the basement. The door is unlocked." Maybe if I show her more of who I am and what I am doing, it will make her feel better. Not just now, but when we finally truly meet face to face.

"I'm walking there now. Will you stay on the phone with me?" Her voice has a little plea in it.

"Of course."

"Why do you believe that seeing your face or hearing your name would upset me so much?" Her footsteps click down the hall.

"There are many things that I haven't told you about myself yet. I'm trying to correct some of that now, but some parts will probably be less acceptable to you than others."

"If you're disfigured or something, I really don't care." She sounds so earnest. But I actually have to laugh a little.

"No, no. It's nothing like that. I protect my identity because of my fame and all the enemies I have managed to amass over the years. I needed to know once and for all that I could trust you," I say. "Last night, you had every reason to sneak a look at my face, but you did not. You truly proved that to me. It made me very happy, Carolyn."

"You don't love someone by ignoring him when he asks you not to do something." Her voice is so gentle.

My heart skips a beat and I have to close my eyes. The feeling that washes over me is exquisite and so intense and unfamiliar that I barely know how to process it. My response is slow and a little breathless.

"You don't love someone by keeping her in the dark either. I'm sorry, Carolyn. But perhaps when you see the nerve center of my home and learn a few things, you will understand why I am so very careful." Please understand.

Her boot heels tap down the stairs leading down into the basement, and then the steps echo a little as she walks through that short hallway. "What's down here?"

"My life's work. Something that I want very much for you to be a part of."

99

She opens the door to the computer hub and catches her breath. "Wow."

That puts a smile on my face. "Please sit down at the main terminal."

"Is that a quantum computer?" My chair creaks as she settles into it.

"Yes. I use a combination of quantum computing, parallel processing clusters, and multiple advanced AI to do my work online. Have a look." Triggering a command on my phone causes the main computer terminal to unlock.

She leans forward to peer at the screen. "And what is your work exactly?"

"Saving people. Protecting communities. Undoing some of the damage that my fellow wealthy and powerful people have done to the world." Deep breath. "Please have a look at the numerical readout on the wall."

She looks. "That's a big number. It just jumped up by three. What is it?"

"That is the number of human beings whose lives, businesses, families, and communities I have positively intervened in since I began working on this project over twenty years ago." My heart swells a little with pride as her eyes light up.

"Then you don't work for that underground league owner in Detroit?"

Another small chuckle escapes me. "No. I own that ring."

She catches her breath. "Then ... I almost saw you."

"Yes. It was very tempting to meet with you in Detroit. These feelings for you are not new. I just thought it was necessary to deny them."

"I'm glad that you didn't," she murmurs tenderly, and that same wonderful feeling rises up in me again.

"So am I. But, dear Carolyn, before I can finally reveal everything to you, we have to stop Assante."

I activate the screen in front of her, and she turns to look at it as I watch her through the computer's camera. She watches raptly as I show her all the different search routines currently running, searching through images from every single internet-connected camera in all of Baltimore, looking for Assante.

She gasps. "This is incredible. There really hasn't been any sign of him?"

"No. Not yet. He may be using a disguise, or he may have found a way to avoid every possible camera so far. He may simply be indoors somewhere without a feed. The hunt has only started. I still do some work with certain members of the underworld community for a price, mind you. But generally, we are allies, or they work for me. Right now, I am mobilizing every asset that I have in Baltimore to look for Assante. This includes enlisting the aid of DuBois." With good fortune, that will be the last lie that I ever have to tell her.

She sits back, her eyes widening. "You have control of DuBois?"

A mischievous smile tugs at my lips. Good thing she can't see it. "Yes. In a manner of speaking."

"Good." Her eyes are still very red, but she surprises me by smiling. "I'm starting to understand how you can know and control so much. This setup is incredible. What you're doing is incredible."

"It pleases me that you think so. It's important to me that you believe in what I am doing." I have to stop and tug at the crotch of my trousers to give myself some room. These wonderful, alien feelings are having a powerful effect on my body.

"I'll tell you what. Help me catch Assante. After that, maybe we can talk about working together more directly." That wonderful determination is back in her voice.

Despite everything, she stands strong. That's part of why I love her so much.

"There is the possibility of laying a trap for him." I use my phone to open a copy of the layout of the Mermaid Club on the screen in front of her. "But, my dear, that would require you to act as the bait. Not my first choice, but if the search of the city can't catch him, drawing him to you might be our only option."

"I know." She doesn't sound worried, just focused. "The Mermaid Club downtown is the only lead Daniels has on where I'll be in the next few days. He knows I'm going there Saturday night to try and talk to DuBois."

She's always surprising me. "You're not concerned about the risks?"

She scoffs. "Of course I am. Assante is far more intelligent and dangerous then Daniels. But it doesn't worry me anywhere near as much, because I trust you. I will draw Assante in, and you will keep me safe and help me catch him." She is looking very intently at the floorplan for the club. "If I can lead him into the service area, I can get him away from any staff and civilians."

"That area is mostly concrete and metal. It would be much easier to contain a firefight there. DuBois can easily set up an ambush for the man there as well. It's a good choice." My breath keeps catching in my chest. My heart and body burn with a growing need for her.

She's not only cooperating, but she was already considering the same plan. She has anticipated me, instead of balking.

She relaxes a little more and smiles a little wider. "It's a good plan. If Assante can't be found by Saturday night, I'll be ready to go through with it."

"My brave Carolyn," I murmur. "Come upstairs."

She catches her breath. "What?"

"Come upstairs. Come to the top floor and to the master bedroom at the end of the hall. You need to have your mind off all of this for a while—and I need you."

102

"I'll be right there." She stands at once. She hangs up and hurries out, vanishing from the view of the camera.

I set the phone down on the nightstand and flip a switch next to my bed. My hours are so erratic thanks to my work that I had light-blocking shutters installed to help me sleep. As they slide down into place, the room is plunged into total darkness.

I take off my clothes and set them on the bedside chair. I roll a condom onto my throbbing, aching penis, the slight stimulation enough to make me pant in my excitement. Then I step back behind my looming bed and wait.

She taps at the door, and I call out calmly, "Come in and close it behind you."

Light spills into the room briefly as she comes in. She closes the door obediently, and then goes a step farther and locks it. "I'm here."

"Take your clothes off."

I hear rustling. The rasp of a zipper. The thump of her shoes being removed. A shudder of anticipation runs through me.

She's starting to breathe harder. "It's done."

"Come over to the bed."

Her feet thump softly on the hardwood floor. I follow the sound, moving around the bed to reach her. I find her standing at the edge of the bed with her back to me, already shaking and breathing hard.

I move up behind her, my voice deep with desire. "In all my life, I have never wanted anyone as much as I want you. I would do anything to keep you."

She turns and throws herself into my arms, fitting herself against me deliciously. Our kissing is rough this time, desperate, her mouth chasing mine as she rubs herself against me. I wrap my arms around her hips, lifting her against me, and then settle her back on the edge of the bed.

I'm learning her body. The spot just below her earlobe where she likes to be kissed. The way that running my tongue around the sides of her nipples make her tremble and pant. How delicately she needs her clitoris stroked.

By the time I enter her, she's whimpering with every breath, her whole body taut under me as it embraces me. I hold still, stroking her gently, ignoring my own need to move. "There, my darling. Now come for me."

Her whimper grows into desperate pants as I stroke her clitoris faster and faster. "It's too good—too good—" she gasps, squirming under me and digging her heels against the side of the bed.

"Take it." My hoarse whisper brims over with heat. "Don't you fight me. Let go."

She arches her back and screams, pushing her hips up against me and grinding hard as her muscles contract around me. "Yes ... yes!"

I seize her hips and start pounding into her, each thrust driving a sharp cry from her as she clutches me closer. My mind fogs over; my whole body thrums with lust and pleasure as her blissful cries go on and on.

"Oh, good girl, good girl. I'm so pleased with you." Then words fail me. My muscles tighten as I draw near a climax so strong that my groans and shouts drown out hers as she starts grinding against me again.

"I love you," she whispers as I rocket toward my explosion. "I love you."

Unfamiliar bliss overwhelms me again; I arch my back and shudder with joy, heart and body feeding each other's pleasure until my climax makes me writhe. My release builds, each long wave roaring through me harder as I empty myself, until my mind empties, too, and the world goes away for a while.

CHAPTER 12

Carolyn

*U*nfortunately for us, all the searches come up short. For three days, we wait for results while Prometheus teaches me about himself and his organization, and at night, makes love to me in a completely darkened room.

I'm both fiercely in love now and also fiercely angry. My colleagues should not have died like this. Nobody should die like this, except perhaps for Assante himself.

I still wonder about what secrets Prometheus is keeping from me. I understand now that he does nothing without a good reason, but it frustrates me not to know everything.

Once Saturday night comes, I resign myself to the inevitable. Prometheus has reassured me that the club will be full of armed people who will descend on my would-be assassin like the fist of an angry god. So, I put on my new blue dress, put my 9mm Walther in my thigh holster underneath it, and put on a sapphire pendant that Prometheus has gifted me with.

Marissa drives me to the club. "Keep your phone's earpiece in," she advises. "We will be watching you at all times and keeping an eye out for him."

"What about DuBois?" He's barely my problem anymore, but the rumors about his deadly exploits make me worry.

She smirks. "Don't think you have to worry about him too much. He's already been fully informed of the situation."

It's crazy. A week ago, I was planning a trip to this damn club to try and have a prayer of catching him. Now I've got to rely on him for security. I put my phone's earpiece into my ear.

"Well, it sounds like everything is upside down at the FBI. Or at least in that Daniels guy's office." Marissa has a mischievous smile on her face that I don't quite understand. "How many times have you been told things by that office that just aren't true?"

Well, thinking about it... "Too many times."

The club is even more gorgeous inside than my surveillance photos made it out to be. Art deco columns, a mirror-tiled ceiling, a live band, and plush red carpets. It really is a testament to criminal excess, but it's very easy on the eyes.

Two upper-level galleries overlook the dance floor. DuBois's tall form walks to the edge of the railing, his cordial glass in his hand and a white-linen suit adorning his body. His beauty is even more arresting in public—but it can't cast its spell over me anymore.

My heart belongs to another.

He stares down at me with a faint smile on his face. Then he moves over to his table and settles in, watching the proceedings silently as more and more people enter the club.

"You want a drink? I'm heading for the bar." Marissa smiles at me brightly, as if we're here to dance instead of to trap a murderer.

"Go ahead. I'll be fine." I'm not drinking a drop of alcohol until Assante is either captured or dead. But a scan of the rapidly increasing number of patrons shows no familiar faces at all, so ... it may be a while.

I step over to a nearby table and sit down as the crowd thickens, quickly obscuring Marissa from sight as she moves toward the bar. All I have to do is get through tonight, and then Prometheus and I—

There is someone behind me. They move up very quickly, and I stand up at once, starting to turn to deal with whoever it is. Please just be some horny drunk—

There's no chance to look behind me. Instead, something sharp presses against my spine from behind.

I freeze.

"I should thank you for making yourself easy to find," Assante says in my ear. "Time and date prearranged. How very convenient."

The cold hatred in his tone terrifies me. I can't even stop to ask how the hell he got inside without anyone noticing him.

He presses the sharp object a little deeper and then moves it around, until it settles over my kidney. "Walk."

He really didn't waste any time at all. Hopefully someone has noticed this. Where are we going? I look up at the gallery, but DuBois has disappeared back into the crowd, abandoning his table. Damn!

"There's an exit at the back of the bathroom hallway. I have disabled the alarm. We'll use it to leave." He pokes me again. "Get moving."

"Why don't you just stab me here in front of witnesses," I suggest. "You've already gotten sloppy. You had no problem shooting a child on a public beach. Or six innocent people in front of security cameras."

He scoffs. "Do you think I don't know who owns this club, child? I will be shot down in under a minute if your death becomes a public spectacle. But if that happens, special agent, I won't be dying alone.

"Let me put it another way. Either you come along quietly and go out that door, or I will empty the pistol I'm carrying into the crowd." His voice is starting to shake; he means it.

"I'm going." My voice is leveler than his. I have to trust that someone is still watching me. Even if I'm going out the wrong door, even if we're going away from the ambush that has been set up, I trust that Prometheus will send someone to help.

The bathroom hallway is long and polished with a fire exit at the far end. I walk with that blade against my kidney, and he talks quietly the entire time.

"It's uncertain how you thought that you could get away with forcing me to suffer such indignities. You are an agent of the law, and you must work within the law." He huffs softly and jerks the knife slightly for emphasis. "You kidnapped me from Mexico! And I'm certain duct tape isn't an accepted form of restraint for a prisoner either."

"If you think those are indignities, maybe you should think about the implications of letting Derek Daniels turn you into an attack dog. You may be a murderer, but that guy is beneath you. Do you have any idea why he's after me?" Talk fast. Maybe something will get through and buy me time.

"He claims you have too much incriminating information on him. It's a common reason why an assassination is called out." He's unimpressed.

Press on. There's nothing to lose. "Do you know that the only reason I have incriminating information on him is because of his repeated efforts to get me killed because I wouldn't sleep with him? This is the man you're cooperating with."

He withdraws the knife just a little. "Really? That is regrettable. Perhaps I should pay him a visit once I'm done with you."

"Honestly, if you took him out, I would almost forgive you for shanking me." That's not entirely honest, but it clearly amuses him enough to finally distract him.

He slows his walk a little. "I can't be as forgiving as you are, sadly. Your offenses against me are too grave."

We've almost reached the door. I know he's going to kill me almost as soon as we're outside. I don't know if I can get to my gun fast enough to defend myself.

"Well, for what it's worth, if I could do it all again, I wouldn't have duct taped you and put you in my trunk. And I'm not just saying that because you're an inch from removing one of my kidneys." No idea how I'm staying so calm when I'm about three paces from death.

Prometheus, where are you?

"You wouldn't?" He actually stops for the moment. "Why not?"

I stop and look back at him over my shoulder. His head is tilted; his face is covered in prosthetic makeup, making him look younger, paler … uglier. If not for those chocolate brown eyes and his voice, it would be impossible to recognize him.

"It's really simple. You're too goddamn dangerous. I should have shot you instead." My smile is full of venom.

He chuckles, bizarrely satisfied by my answer. "That would have at least been treating me with the respect and fear I deserve. Now, why don't you go out that door, and we'll conclude our business."

That's when the lights go out.

The hallway is suddenly plunged into darkness, and I throw myself to the side. I hear his knife slide against the steel door that was behind me and fumble for my gun in the dark. Then sudden, rapid footsteps come up on us; there's a thud, and Assante gasps aloud.

The lights come back on as Assante's knife slips from his fingers and clatters to the floor. He is standing rigidly not four feet away from me, his fingers splayed out, his eyes wide and a look of shock on his face. He's letting out little choking noises instead of breathing, and instead of his eyes being empty, they're full of genuine surprise.

A moment later, his knees buckle, and he falls to the side, that expression still frozen on his face. His collapse reveals the man standing behind him: DuBois, a single drop of blood on his cheek, a look of absolute fury on his beautiful face.

His expression softens as our eyes meet, and he looks at me with relief as I stare back at him in shock. I look down and see the thin silver handle of a stiletto protruding from the base of Assante's skull.

"Are you all right?" DuBois pants in Prometheus's voice.

What?

I explode. "You? This is who you are?"

The fifth name on Daniels's list. Not an associate of Prometheus or someone he wanted to use, but Prometheus himself.

I understand at once why he hid it from me, and why he hides it from everyone. But that doesn't make it any less of a shock. I back toward the door.

"I'm sorry for deceiving you." He reaches toward me pleadingly with bloody hands. "Please forgive me."

My back bumps against the steel door. It's too much. Maybe it wouldn't be if I wasn't in love with him. Maybe it wouldn't be if I wasn't already overwhelmed. But I'm both, and I can't take it. "Who are you really?" I demand. "Is everything you said to me a lie?"

"No! Don't go," he pleads. "If you walk out of my life, you take my heart with you. You're the only woman I've ever loved."

His words only put a small dent in my anger. "And yet you're willing to lie to me this much? When will it end?" My hand is on the latch to the door. "How do I know you won't just keep deceiving me?"

"It ends now," he murmurs in that tender voice. "Please, Carolyn, don't leave. I'll tell you anything you want. I'll show you anything you want. But don't walk away."

Even terrified, even watching him wipe the blood off his hands with a wet nap and dab that single red droplet off his cheek, there is no denying it. His desperation moves me.

"Did you use me to get the Don of New York killed?" I look him right in the eyes, and he glances away.

"Yes."

"How could you treat me like that? I'm not your toy!" I glance down at Assante again. The only reason I'm not walking out that door right now is because Prometheus—Adrian—just saved my life again.

"At the time, you were simply another FBI agent in a situation I sympathized with. I needed that man to die to protect my family and his daughter. You were one of the people in the right position to help make that happen. That's all."

Finally, some straight answers. "What about the rest of the list? Did you have a hand in it somehow?"

He relaxes slightly, as if understanding that if I'm asking questions, I'm still listening to the answers.

"Yes. I did. And I am sorry for failing to divulge that to you." His smile is more like a grimace. "You see, Derek Daniels wanted to give you a much different list, one which would have led you to unwittingly go toe-to-toe with cop killers without backup."

He takes a deep breath. "I deceived him and altered the list. Instead, I made sure the men you were chasing were the sort who would never hurt you. Even when I didn't know you, I still sympathized. Now, I love you more than my own life. I beg you not to throw your trust in me away. Please." The pain in his eyes, the raw vulnerability, frightens me in its own way just as much as the man on the floor used to.

Is it possible I could destroy someone this powerful just by walking away? I close my eyes and lean my back against the door, tears trickling out from under my lashes.

I worked myself to the bone to become an FBI agent. And once I did, every step of the way, my superior there did everything in his power to make sure I would fail, suffer, and die. The man in front of me is inviting me to leave them and join him in dispensing his own brand of justice and mercy in the world.

And even with blood on his hands and all these lies, he's still more trustworthy, and he gets better results.

And I love him.

I open my eyes and look into his. "I don't want to leave." I watch him sag with relief. "But if you ever deceive me like this again, I will."

He looks away from me, blinking rapidly, his eyes suspiciously bright for just a moment. "I swear I will never give you reason to distrust me again."

"Then that's good enough for now." This relationship is going to need a lot of work.

But as I calm down, I'm hopeful. Unlike my time with the FBI, with Prometheus, I'll be listened to. I'll be able to make real progress.

I look down at the crumpled corpse. Rest in pieces, you soulless bastard. "What do we do with him?"

He is quiet for a moment and then smirks slightly. "Just leave that to me. I already have something in mind."

He moves past the body and takes me in his arms. "Do you need a drink before we leave? The bartender mixes lovely cocktails."

"No," I say honestly, nestling my cheek against his chest. His heart is beating fast, and I marvel again at how much power I have over such an amazing man.

"No, I don't need a drink. I just need you." He nuzzles the top of my head in response to my words, and I murmur against his throat, "Let's go home."

THE END.

EPILOGUE

Derek

*I*t's been three weeks and I have radio silence from both Carolyn Moss and from that damn assassin Assante. I thought that bastard was a professional, but it seems like he's taken his freedom and my money. Aside from the big damn mess at the hotel, he didn't do a thing in return.

I'm still healing from the beating Assante gave me, too. I told that bastard to make his escape look realistic, and in return, I got two black eyes, twenty stitches, and some dental work.

Shit, I guess that's realistic enough to throw off suspicions. But the least he can do is get the damn job done before he vanishes.

If any of Moss's sisters know what's going on with her, they aren't saying anything. Nor has Assante returned to Las Vegas as far as anyone in the Vegas FBI knows. The two of them could have been abducted by aliens for all the trace that they have left.

Nevertheless, I haven't completely lost out. Carolyn's disappearance has had the chilling effect on the other women in the office that I hoped it would. The investigation is still going on, but the girls are being a lot less cooperative.

Assante's murder of the four FBI agents who I assigned to Moss in Baltimore had an equal benefit. Now, there are no more witnesses left who know about the transmitters I had those poor boys plant in Moss's hotel room.

I dodged a serious bullet on that one.

Sitting in my office, staring down at the cardboard box with the contents of her desk in it, I still feel like I've won. She has completely disappeared off my radar. That means she can't cause me any more trouble.

There's still the possibility that she'll pop back up in the hospital or something, but I don't think so. I've already put in for a brand-new crop of agents to fill the empty seats in my office. In a couple of months, it will be like Carolyn Moss never existed in my life.

"I'll drink to that," I say to myself, scooping the box off my desk and shoving it into the far corner of my office. I'll keep it for a month or so in case one of her sisters pops up wanting her stuff. That's how nice a guy I am.

Besides, they're probably as hot as she is, and there's no way that every one of them is an uppity shrew.

I'm starting to pack up for the day when a late package comes in by courier. The receptionist has already gone home, so the janitor brings it in. "The guy just left it with your name on it," he says quietly.

It's a pretty big box. It could hold a soccer ball or something. It's a little heavier than that, though.

I look it over and notice that it is postmarked from Las Vegas. Nothing on the packaging to indicate who exactly sent it. However, I only know one guy who has dealings with me who might be in Vegas right now.

Maybe I've had it wrong. Maybe Assante is sending me proof he finally finished the job. I look around, making sure I'm alone in the office except for that pesky janitor, who is already gone back to his work. Then I eagerly start ripping the tape off the package.

My email indicator dings. I look up at my screen, and notice that I'm being CC'd on a document delivery that's being sent to the section director and his immediate superior. I don't recognize the email address that it's being sent from, but it looks official.

A cold breath of fear blows on the back of my neck.

Quickly, I turn to my computer and open up the email. There's a brief note and a series of attachments. The note says simply, **RE Derek Daniels** and my guts loosen.

What is going on?

I open the attachments and start going through them quickly. My eyes widen in horror as I realize what they contain.

Private emails. Private texts. Conversations, negotiations, and threats that I never wanted to see the light of day. CCTV footage of me unlocking Assante's handcuffs and letting him go.

Sick, cold, my heart beating way too fast, I sit back from my desk, realizing that it's over. No way of knowing exactly who sent this, but my guess is, it was Carolyn Moss again. But that makes even less sense, considering the package on my desk.

I turn to the package and finish tearing it open. Inside is one of those tiny foam coolers full of dry ice that are used to deliver things like meat or fancy cheeses. That piques my curiosity.

Maybe it's a completely unrelated gift. But who the hell else do I know in Vegas besides Assante?

I hastily pull the top off the cooler and a thick mist swirls up from the dry ice. A lot of it has already boiled off. It's pretty warm in Vegas this week.

It still takes me a moment for the mist to clear and for me to get a good look at what's inside. Then I have to stifle a scream.

Assante's face stares back at me, ice crystals covering the lenses of his glasses, his expression startled, like he can't believe someone finally got the drop on him.

"Oh God," I wheeze. "She's a fucking monster!"

The realization that I underestimated Carolyn Moss comes way too late.

That's when the door opens, and multiple feet walk toward my office.

She called them ahead of time. Suspicions filling my head, I grab the box and its grisly contents, desperately looking around for a place to hide it.

"Right over here, sir," the janitor cheerfully says as I try to jam the box into a drawer that's too small for it.

That's how the section director finds me as he steps into the doorway: frantic, endless evidence against me glowing on my computer screen, and the box with Assante's severed head still in my hands.

THE END.

ABOUT THE AUTHOR

Mrs. Love writes about smart, sexy women and the hot alpha billionaires who love them. She has found her own happily ever after with her dream husband and adorable 6 and 2 year old kids. Currently, Michelle is hard at work on the next book in the series, and trying to stay off the Internet.

"Thank you for supporting an indie author. Anything you can do, whether it be writing a review, or even simply telling a fellow reader that you enjoyed this. Thanks

Printed by BoD™ in Norderstedt, Germany